The E-Team

Project Mogul

Tim Trott

Tim Trott Publishing

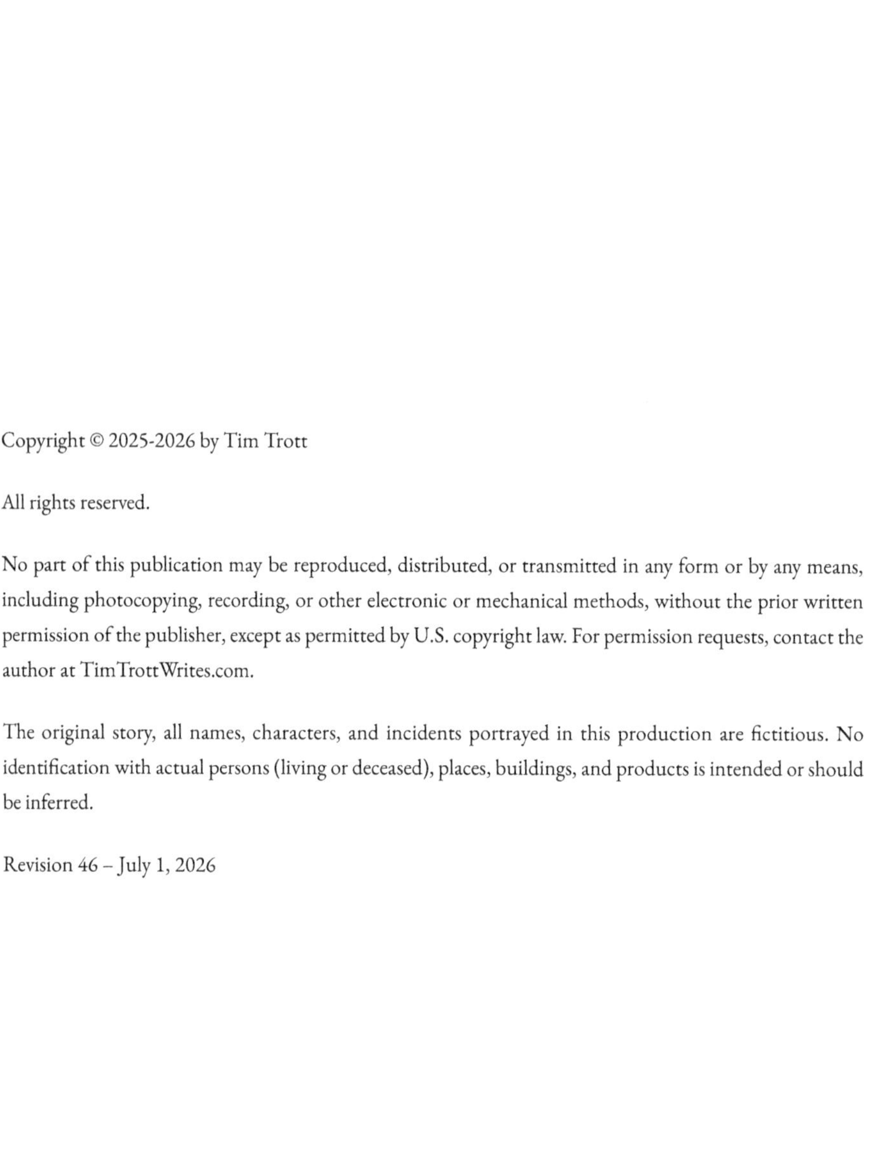

Revision 46 – July 1, 2026

Contents

Acknowledgements

The author wishes to express deep appreciation to the members of the Daytona Writers Group and the many beta readers and whose thoughtful critiques and observations helped strengthen this story.

Chapter One

Javelin and the Ghost

High over the Syrian-Turkish border, an Air Force CV-22 Osprey's mission was a high-speed, low-level insertion to drop off a team of Air Force Combat Controllers to a dusty landing zone, just inside the friendly Kurdish sector.

At the controls was the seasoned pilot, Captain Russ "Javelin" Garner, dark-haired and compact, with the kind of stillness that came from having done this a hundred times and never quite trusting the hundred-and-first. On his left sat co-pilot Captain John Miller.

They nicknamed the aircraft 'The Ghost,' a name that would soon prove fitting.

In the cabin behind the cockpit was the four-man combat team with their gear.

It was nightfall by the time they reached their destination.

The insertion was quick and professional. Captain Garner set the Osprey into a low hover and lowered the ramp. The first two operators went down the ramp and onto the ground, carrying their heavy packs. They surveyed the situation and waved back at the crew chief, and the last two members of the team joined them on the ground. The crew chief signaled a "thumbs-up" to Captain Garner. The ramp closed, and the Osprey lifted away as the heavily laden team disappeared into the night.

The entire process took less than a minute.

The mission was simple, but it unraveled within seconds.

The AWACS controller's voice delivered the first warning.

"Vagabond 2-1, be advised, comms traffic in your area indicates possible air defense activity."

Captain Garner scanned the horizon as the jagged brown ridges slid below at 250 knots. Just then, an alarm screamed for attention.

"Radar lock! SA-22 'Greyhound'. Pantsir-S1." Miller's voice tightened. "Bearing zero-niner-zero at our altitude. They've got us. What are the options?"

Garner's hand tightened on the cyclic. He knew the SA-22 Pantsir's dual-tracking would ignore his flares; standard countermeasures were useless against a system that could see him even when its radar couldn't lock.

"Flares and chaff won't cut it. That's what they're expecting. Hold on. We're about to violate the hell out of the flight manual."

Normal procedure would have called for the pilot to dive or turn away. But Captain Garner did what the manual said not to do. He pulled back on the aft cyclic, pitching the Osprey's nose up in a sharp, energy-bleeding climb. At the same time, his left hand slammed the nacelle control, which forced the massive rotors to shift from aircraft to helicopter mode. Loose gear floated through the cabin in a near zero-G moment.

The aircraft groaned in protest as the sudden deceleration jerked both pilots forward against their harnesses.

"We're stalling!" yelled Miller as the blare of the stall warning rendered his protest redundant.

Before the Osprey could fully stall, Garner reversed the process, shoving the nacelles forward, dipping the plane's nose down. The turbine engines screamed as they grabbed the air, and the Osprey dropped like a stone into the radar shadow of a deep ravine.

The G-force pressed the crew back into their seats.

"Lock broken, missile gone!" Miller's voice was still shaking.

Garner leveled the aircraft without answering.

"Vagabond 2-1 to AWACS, we encountered a ..." He paused. "Navigational anomaly. Proceeding to alternate LZ."

AWACS replied simply, "Acknowledged." Both pilots knew what had nearly happened, but nobody wanted to say it aloud. The repercussions were yet to come.

A week after the incident, Captain Russ Garner was flown back to Kadena Air Base in Okinawa, Japan, for a debrief. He stood at attention in the office of Colonel E. Vance, 353rd Special Operations Wing. The aircraft Garner had put through "Dip and Zip" calisthenics was one of the Ospreys assigned to the wing.

The senior officers were not impressed.

Garner remained standing as the officer slid a sheet of paper across the desk.

"The official report says in-flight emergency necessitating an unconventional recovery maneuver to preserve airframe and crew. I call that a masterpiece of fiction. We know what really happened, don't we?"

"Sir, I responded to a direct threat to my aircraft and crew."

"That 'Dip and Zip' stunt isn't in the Dash-1. Every flight model says you should have left your wings in the dirt over Syria." Vance's cold stare bore into Garner's face. "You got lucky. I would say, incredibly lucky. But in my wing, luck is not a sustainable operational doctrine."

Garner remained silent. He knew every system on the aircraft. There was nothing to say.

Colonel Vance leaned forward. "Your tour is concluded. Effective immediately, you are transferred stateside to Edwards Air Force Base for simulator instruction duties."

"Sir, I ..." He realized protest was pointless.

"Dismissed, Captain."

As he left the building, Garner headed to the BX, hoping to shake off what he was feeling in a cup of coffee, or something stronger.

"Captain Garner?"

Garner turned to see a man in a crisp civilian suit, standing next to a black government sedan.

"Who's asking?"

"You can call me Mr. Smith. That's no matter. I'm with a ... liaison group from the Department of the Air Force. We have a proposition for you." He gestured to the car. "A short drive? Somewhere we can speak privately?"

Every instinct said keep walking. He stopped anyway. The demotion was already issued; whatever this was couldn't make it worse. He got into the car, expecting to be taken to another office on base. Instead, he was driven to a private hangar on the far side of the flightline.

Inside the bare space were a small table and two chairs.

"We studied the telemetry from your incident," Smith began without preamble. "The maneuver you executed was certainly not luck, Captain. It was genius, showing a level of instinctive, fluid understanding of your aircraft. They can't teach that in flight school because it comes from experience. Colonel Vance could not appreciate that, but what you have is the very thing we need."

Garner studied the man for a moment before asking, "Who is 'we'?"

Smith responded, "We are a group that operates beyond the standard chain of command. We deal with the kind of problems that, if they became public, would make your recent border incident look like a diplomatic spat. If you are interested, we have an opening for a pilot with your specific talents. A permanent transfer."

Smith let the last two words hang: 'permanent transfer.'

"To where?"

"You might say to a place that does not exist," Smith replied with a knowing smile. "You'll be flying a significantly modified platform, an improved version of the Osprey. The mission profile will make your work here seem like an airline route."

"What's the mission?"

"It could be described as preserving a truth that would redefine human history. May I assume you are interested?"

Garner's eyes swept across the vastness of the empty building.

Here was a chance to avoid a career death sentence. But it was also a leap into something unknown: a shadow organization, unaccountable chains of command, missions that would never make it into official reports. Everything his academy training had warned him against.

He thought of what was waiting for him if he walked away. The reassignment to simulator instruction. The end of a flying career.

It was an easy choice. It just didn't feel like one.

"What is the next step?"

"You sign some papers." From a drawer in the desk, Smith produced a thick stack of documents bound with a security seal. "Your new home is Groom Lake. Welcome to Project Mogul."

Before Garner could speak, Smith added, "Officially, that program ended in '49, but some government programs don't really end."

***

Ten hours later, Russ Garner was aboard a commercial flight from Okinawa to Las Vegas, sipping bad coffee over the Pacific. The man who introduced himself as Mr. Smith had provided a first-class ticket and a new identity as "Robert Evans." His instructions were to go to the south terminal of McCarran Airport and find the US Air Force ticket counter.

In Vegas, the desert air hit him like a blast furnace. Following the instructions, he moved through the crowds of tourists and found the small, unassuming counter in a secluded part of the airport. A plain blue-and-white sign read "JANET." The woman behind the counter wore a typical airline uniform, but her posture was ramrod straight.

"May I help you, sir?" she asked as he approached.

"Robert Evans. I believe I have a reservation." He slid his new ID across the counter.

The clerk scrolled a digital tablet and responded with a curt nod. "Gate S7. The aircraft will be boarding in ten minutes. Have a pleasant flight."

There was no ticket, no boarding pass, only a gesture from the clerk pointing to a door marked "AUTHORIZED PERSONNEL ONLY".

A dozen people waited at Gate S7, mostly a mix of men and women in civilian clothes. No one made small talk. No one looked at their phones. Garner assumed they were engineers, scientists, or security personnel.

Outside the gate, the aircraft taxied into view exactly on schedule. The stark, unadorned white Boeing 737 had a single red stripe running the length of its fuselage. There was a tail number N319BD, but no airline logo, only the lettering "JANET" in all caps below the cockpit window, identifying the covert shuttle to America's most secure base.

On board the plane, the flight was short and silent. The flight attendants looked more like a security detail: broad-shouldered men in dark suits. They offered no drinks or snacks.

The plane passed over the neon sprawl of Las Vegas to the vast emptiness of the Nevada desert until it reached a cluster of runways and buildings. The official name of the airfield at Area 51 is Homey Airport, but there were no signs making that identification as the plane rolled to a stop at a hangar. Passengers disembarked onto the hot tarmac where a base shuttle bus idled nearby, its windows completely blacked out. A driver in coveralls stood by the door.

"Evans, Robert," the driver said, not as a question. Garner acknowledged with a raised index finger and boarded. He sat alone in the dimly lit interior of the bus and monitored the scene through the windshield as the other passengers boarded another bus at the entrance to the hangar.

The driver boarded, took his position, and the door hissed shut.

"Just you and me, Captain," the driver said as he put the bus in gear and pulled away from the hangar.

Garner's fingers tightened on the duffel strap. "Where are we going?"

"Your new office: S-3."

Garner frowned. "Don't you mean S-4?"

The driver chuckled as he glanced at the captain's reflection in the mirror. "Your clearance is for S-3."

The bus picked up speed as it followed a dirt road that snaked into the foothills until it seemed to be headed straight for a solid rock face. The road made a sharp turn into a narrow canyon. As they approached, a large section of rock and scrub slid sideways, revealing a massive door seamlessly integrated into the mountain.

Inside, the bus pulled into a colossal cavern, illuminated by banks of overhead lights, as the closing of the hangar door rumbled behind them.

***

What caught Garner's attention under the brilliant glow of spotlights was a familiar sight. It was a V-22 like no Osprey he had ever seen. Its skin was radar-absorbent black, devoid of any insignia. He noted that the engine nacelles were slightly more angular.

The bus pulled to a stop. The driver opened the door and turned in his seat.

"Welcome home, Captain. Go through that door and they'll set you up with your new living quarters."

He picked up his gear and went through the door. He had no way of knowing what lay ahead.

Chapter Two

The Challenge

The corridor in Containment Block C ran two hundred feet without a window, lit by panels that hummed faintly at a frequency most people never noticed. Kaela Renn noticed it every time. She had worked in this facility long enough to know every sound it made and what each one meant.

She stopped outside the door to Room 3. Through the reinforced glass panel, the being on the other side of the room was still. It had not moved in six hours, according to the log. The overnight staff had noted elevated readings on the biometric sensors but had not gone in. They rarely did.

Renn set her clipboard on the shelf beside the door and looked through the glass.

The being looked back.

That was the part the staff found unsettling. It always seemed to know when someone was watching, regardless of where it was in the room or whether the lights were up. It would orient toward the observation panel with those large dark eyes and simply wait, as though it had already determined that patience was the only available strategy.

Kaela Renn understood that, in some ways she could not have explained to her supervisor or to the committee that reviewed her file annually, she understood it completely.

She keyed her access card and went inside.

Renn worked as an assistant to the administrator of the modest medical facility at Groom Lake, the advanced flight test and development base run by the U.S. Air Force, known as Area 51. She later became the facility's business administrator, bringing more than just her MBA to the role. Her late mother had been a nurse, and Kaela was born at that same facility. Her most important qualification was one the job description could never name.

In October 1975, a craft of unknown origin was recovered near Prescott, Arizona, with two occupants. One was deceased; the other critically injured but alive. The military secretly transported the surviving alien, the "Extraterrestrial Biological Entity," or EBE, to the Area 51 facility.

One night, the twenty-one-year-old Kaela, working as an assistant while attending college, felt a sensation that compelled her through a corridor to Containment Room 3. When her eyes met those of the alien creature restrained inside, something opened in her that she had no language for, a flood of sensation that sent her to her knees in the corridor before she understood what was happening. It took weeks before she could manage the contact without physical cost. It took months before she could hold a coherent exchange.

Over time, that raw and overwhelming first connection became something she could control, and she became the facility's primary human-alien communicator. Restrained inside, she discovered she could sense its thoughts, its fear, and its desperate attempt to communicate. She refined this telepathic ability to become the facility's primary human-alien communicator. When the entity was eventually returned in a negotiated exchange, Kaela's role as a bridge between species was firmly established.

Over the following decades, she became a vital asset in the government's extraterrestrial relations. Her Nordic hybrid biology meant that the passing years left fewer marks on her than on her peers. While those around her grew old, she looked much the same as she had twenty years before. Her slowed maturation allowed her to serve as a consistent point of contact for the visitors, speaking for both sides across multiple human generations.

A few years later, there was a knock on the open doorway to her office. She looked up to see a man she didn't recognize. He was lean in the way that suggested years of physical discipline rather than any particular habit. His dark business suit was unremarkable, the kind typically worn by a mid-level government official.

"Miss Renn," he said from the doorway. "I need to speak with you privately."

She set down the file she had been working on, studying him. "And you are?"

"You can call me Mr. Smith." He remained in the doorway. "May I close the door?"

His tone was professional and carried no threat, and she nodded. Years of dealing with classified projects had taught her to recognize situations above standard clearance levels.

"I represent certain interests; interests that operate outside the standard chain of command. We have been aware of your work for some time. Your special qualities have not gone unnoticed."

Kaela leaned back, her expression cautious.

"I'm listening. Where are we going with this?" she asked.

"A certain faction is shooting down alien craft to harvest technology. The situation is deteriorating rapidly. We need someone who can operate outside those channels, someone the aliens might actually trust."

Smith set a single sheet of paper on the desk between them. A list of three incidents, each with a date, a location, and a terse description of what had been recovered. He did not explain them. He did not need to.

Renn read it twice. She set it down.

"You're describing a program that doesn't exist," she said.

"That's correct."

"Reporting to no one I've ever heard of."

"Also correct."

She looked at the paper again without picking it up. The third incident was six weeks ago. She had heard the base rumor about the radar anomaly over Nellis. Now she understood what the rumor was covering.

"What happens if I say no?"

"We find someone else," Smith said. "Though I think you know there isn't anyone else."

The room was quiet. Somewhere in the corridor outside, a cart rolled past and the sound faded.

Renn folded her hands on the desk. "I'll need the right people. Proper resources. A secure facility and complete operational autonomy. No Pentagon oversight, no second-guessing after the fact. If I accept this, I run it my way."

Smith produced a handwritten note from his jacket pocket and placed it on the desk beside the paper. A phone number, nothing else.

"Think about it," he said. "Call when you're ready."

She made that call the next morning. Two days later, she found herself in an unmarked building, facing a committee that would change everything.

***

The building had no marked address. Inside was a conference room that was equally anonymous, with beige walls, fluorescent lighting, and a table surrounded by office chairs that could have come from any government surplus catalog. The only unusual detail was the absence of windows and the heavy steel door that locked from the inside. A world map covered a large portion of one wall.

As Kaela entered, the three people at the table stopped mid-conversation. Even in the sterile fluorescent light of the windowless room, Kaela drew attention by her appearance. Her height allowed her to look most of the men in the eye, and her blonde hair and piercing blue eyes caused one member to shift in his chair as she crossed the room.

The apparent leader of the group introduced herself to Kaela as Major Lila Chen and tapped her pen against her tablet as she addressed the group. She was precise, military-sharp, someone used to giving orders.

"The situation is becoming critical."

A balding man in a plain dark suit, whom the others referred to as Croft, cleared his throat. "The public's demanding disclosure..."

Another of the group, wearing a Marine uniform with a name tag that identified him as Major Arlis Thorne, leaned forward and added, "The old standard of denial, disinformation, and distraction is failing."

Kaela Renn listened as she pulled her ponytail through the back of a dark baseball cap. She glanced at the others, still wondering what all this had to do with her.

"The public's yelling for transparency, the military's about to stumble into a fight it can't win, and corporate scavengers are hoping to cash in."

Croft added, "What we need is a rapid-response team that can intercept alien recoveries before the military exploits them, maintain diplomatic contact with visiting species, and prevent incidents that could trigger public disclosure, or worse, an interplanetary conflict. A team that can operate between the official channels and the reality on the ground."

At that point, eyes drifted around the room until they landed on Renn.

Kaela studied the faces of each member of the group as she realized why she was there and the enormity of the challenge she might be facing.

After a moment she said, "I'll need the right people, proper resources, a secure facility, and complete operational autonomy. No bureaucratic oversight, no second-guessing from the Pentagon. If I accept this responsibility, I run it my way."

Thorne pulled out a tablet, selected a photo, and slid it across the table.

Kaela looked at the image of the hidden hangar, a place that felt like a relic from another era. She could almost sense that whatever had been kept here had not fully left. The mountain had held those secrets for decades. It could hold more.

After a moment, Kaela Renn straightened. "I'm ready," she said.

Thorne leaned in, lowering his voice. "You won't find our budget in any congressional hearing. You report to Tier-1. Even the Oval Office hasn't had eyes on this level since Eisenhower."

He glanced around the room. "We're reactivating the Mogul name for operational cover."

Major Chen turned to Renn. "Director Renn, welcome aboard. Welcome to Project Mogul."

***

Several weeks later, a familiar number appeared on Kaela's phone. When she answered, she recognized the voice of Major Arlis Thorne.

"Ready to tour your new assignment?"

"I was hoping to hear from you. When can we leave?"

"Any time you're ready. I'm right outside."

Kaela peered through the window of her apartment to see a black minivan parked outside.

The drive south took them toward the Papoose Mountains, through a narrow gap in rising rock walls. Thorne said little during the drive, but he carried himself like a man who knew every turn of this road.

The gap widened just enough to reveal a cliff face ahead, ordinary at first glance, sun-bleached stone with a scatter of desert brush. The minivan rolled to a stop. Kaela was about to ask what they were waiting for when the cliff shifted. A seam appeared and widened, the entire section folding inward on heavy hinges to reveal a wash of bright white light.

"Even from satellite imagery, it reads as solid rock," Thorne said.

The driver pulled them inside. The cavern swallowed the vehicle, and the door sealed behind them with a heavy thud that resonated through natural stone.

The hangar was compact but purposeful, the ceiling arching overhead in natural stone, smoothed where it needed to be and left raw where it did not. A Bell V-22 Osprey sat near the far wall with its rotors folded. LED fixtures blazed from scaffolding. Workers moved between equipment carts and lift platforms. A welding torch threw sparks that briefly lit the stone above.

"How far does it go?" Kaela asked.

"Eighty meters end to end. The craft program ran here until 1989, then moved to the larger Sector 4 facility when it outgrew the space." He nodded toward the scaffold. "We're nearly finished with the renovation. Your team can be assigned once the final checks clear."

They moved through the rest of the facility at a measured pace: the central corridor lined with fresh conduit and cable bundles, the Ready Room where large screens were being mounted along three walls, and finally the server room, quiet and cold, racks standing empty with cooling fans already whispering.

When they returned to the hangar, the noise washed over them again.

Thorne scanned the space. “It wasn’t abandoned. It was waiting.”

Kaela let the words settle. S-3 was not just a facility coming to life. Something about the cavern suggested it had always known it was temporary storage, not a grave .

“When can I get started?” she asked.

Thorne smiled. “Plan on moving in next week. Let me know where to send the truck.”

Chapter Three

The Prodigal

The wind off Puget Sound cut across the tarmac at Naval Air Station Whidbey Island as Mark Delaney left the Naval Information Warfare Command building.

The assignment was to turn the Russian Internet Research Agency's own infrastructure into a labyrinth of false signals and dead ends. He and his "Ghost Watch" team, the small cyber team he'd handpicked, had fed the Russians false data, sowing internal paranoia, and finally bricking their servers with an elegant malicious code package.

The mission's success was evident in how calm everything remained on U.S. Election Day: no interference, no chaos, no late-night panic from the intelligence community. As Delaney trudged toward the dormitory barracks, the deep "thump-thump-thump" from the rotor blades rolled across the base, so familiar, but it still made him look up. He shaded his eyes against the sun and spotted a V-22 Osprey coming in for a landing, engines tilted up, gliding down soft as a seabird returning to its nest. He'd seen this play out so many times before, but today, for some reason, it hit him differently.

He stopped in his tracks as his thoughts turned to his father, Chief Petty Officer Patrick Delaney.

The senior Delaney served as crew on the MV-22B during Operation Inherent Resolve. He'd come home from deployment with stories of inserting Marines into the Iraqi desert under cover of darkness and resupplying special ops teams in places that don't exist on any public map. The Osprey could accomplish what helicopters couldn't.

Patrick Delaney wanted more than anything to see Mark follow in his footsteps, but computers had always fascinated his son. Mark chose cybersecurity, and he was good at it from the start. Then, shortly after his father returned home for good, a head-on collision with a drunk driver on a rain-slicked interstate ended the discussion.

The sight of that magnificent aircraft brought it all back. His father's dream now felt like an unclaimed inheritance.

Three days later, Lieutenant Mark Delaney stood at attention in the office of Captain Bradley Walsh, still boyish despite the uniform, dark hair regulation-short, the kind of easy-to-overlook face that made him good at his job before anyone taught him to be good at it.

"Delaney, your work on the recent network defense exercise has been noted at the highest levels. You are to be congratulated. You have a remarkable future."

"Thank you, sir," Delaney said, as the officer gestured for him to be at ease. "That means a great deal to me, but I have a request."

"A request?" The captain looked puzzled.

"I'd like to apply for a lateral transfer to naval aviation and go to flight school, sir."

Captain Walsh was silent for a long moment, his eyes searching Mark's face.

"You'll be starting over. Why would you want to walk away from a sure thing?"

The lieutenant didn't blink. "Because, sir, I just proved what I can do in the virtual world, but now I would like to fly the V-22 like my father. It's what he wanted me to do."

Walsh studied him for another moment, then gave a slow nod. "Your father was a good man. Stubborn, as I recall. I see the apple didn't fall far. Alright, Delaney. You've earned a shot. Don't make me regret it."

"Thank you, sir," Delaney responded as he snapped a quick salute.

***

The selection board approved him for Undergraduate Pilot Training on the strength of his performance record, which was an unusual outcome for an officer who had spent his career behind a keyboard. Most of the other candidates had come up through aviation support or tactical operations. Delaney had come up through network defense. The board noted it in his file and approved him.

Flight training nearly broke him. Six months in primary, six in helos, six more learning the Osprey's tilt-rotor quirks, and a security clearance process that dug through every corner of his life.

At 28, Lieutenant Delaney graduated as an Osprey pilot, right on schedule.

He was in the BOQ at NAS Kingsville packing his duffel bag, anticipating a transfer back to Whidbey Island, when his personal phone buzzed.

"Lieutenant Delaney?" a calm voice said.

"Who's calling?" he answered.

"I represent certain interests. We've been watching your progress. Your unique abilities are of great interest. The talent you exhibited before flight school combined with the new skills you now possess make you a singular candidate."

Mark's senses went alert. "Candidate for what?"

"You could say for a mission that does not exist, officially, anyway. But it's a mission at the intersection of everything you know. It's a task that is more important than any network defense. Do I have your interest?"

Mark's thoughts turned to his father, and to that moment on the flight line at Whidbey Island, watching the Osprey come in for a landing.

"I'm listening."

"There is an envelope taped under the bench outside your quarters. Inside you will find a new ID, some cash, and a ticket to Las Vegas. Go to the McCarran private terminal. A ticket for a flight will be waiting. Your current life is going to change. Tell no one."

The call ended, leaving Mark with a silent phone. Part of him wanted to report this immediately to his commanding officer. But another part, the part that had watched that Osprey land at Whidbey Island and felt his father's dream calling to him, recognized something in the caller's tone. This wasn't a scam or a trap.

This was an invitation to something his father would have understood: a mission that lived in the shadows, where the real work got done. His dad had hinted at operations that never made it into after-action reports. Maybe this was Mark's chance to walk the same path.

Thirty-six hours later, the plane with JANET 739, painted in unremarkable white with a simple red stripe, touched down with a squeal of tires on the runway at the Nevada Test and Training Range. The sign at the terminal read "HOMEY AIRPORT (KXTA), Groom Lake, NV".

Mark recognized it as the place the world knows as Area 51.

An Air Force security officer met him and gestured toward a white bus. He climbed aboard, and the bus drove for twenty minutes across the desert. When the bus doors opened, he was inside a cavernous hangar carved into the rock. The air was cool and smelled of ozone and jet fuel.

A man in a flight suit stepped forward. The name tag read GARNER, captain's insignia on his collar.

"Lieutenant Delaney, I'm Captain Russ Garner. We've been expecting you." Garner gestured around the hangar. "Welcome to Project Mogul."

Delaney paused. "Mogul? Like the old weather balloon cover story?"

"That was then; this is now. Sometimes government programs don't really end, they just evolve."

The aircraft parked in the center of the bay drew Mark's eyes. It was an Osprey, but not like the ones he had seen in training. The skin was radar-absorbent black; the angles were sharper; and it featured an array of odd sensors integrated seamlessly into the airframe.

"I see you've noticed Pandora. You'll have a proper introduction later," Garner added.

"Pandora ... as in Pandora's Box? What is this place?" Mark asked, his voice suddenly quiet.

"This," said a fresh voice, "is where your future begins."

They both turned to see a slender woman who moved with an unnatural, fluid grace.

Director Kaela Renn was tall with platinum-blonde hair. She appeared to be in her late forties, but her piercing blue eyes were ageless. To Mark, she looked nearly identical to the decades-old surveillance photos in his father's classified files.

"Lieutenant Delaney," she said, offering a slender hand. Her grip was cool and firm.

"I'm Director Kaela Renn. I've read your background. Your father's service paved the way, but your skills have opened the door. And this," she said, turning to the aircraft, "is Pandora. I wouldn't worry about old myths. What matters is what she can do."

Chapter Four

Pandora

The next morning, Lieutenant Delaney grabbed breakfast early in the dining hall. A few people sat scattered at separate tables. They glanced up, gave him a nod, and went back to their food. Delaney didn't see it as rudeness. In a secure environment, people avoided asking questions, and small talk was discouraged.

He was polishing off a second helping of scrambled eggs and toast when Captain Garner and Director Renn slid into seats across from him.

"So, what's the Plan of the Day?" Delaney asked.

"Today we introduce you to Pandora," Captain Garner said. "We'll need to get you up to speed on some of the special equipment."

"Special equipment? Like what, exactly?"

Renn caught Garner's eye and allowed the corners of her mouth to lift. "I can safely say you're in for a few surprises."

***

After breakfast, Garner led Delaney out to the hangar. In the center sat a V-22 Osprey under a cluster of spotlights.

Except this Osprey was different.

He'd read the specs, but seeing the nacelles up close was different. Each one was a rotating engine pod mounted at the wingtip, the V-22's defining feature: tilt them up and the rotors lifted the aircraft like a helicopter; swing them forward and it flew like a turboprop plane. The transition between the two was where most pilots earned their respect for the aircraft. On Pandora, the nacelle angles were subtly modified from standard, tightened tolerances he could see in the housing geometry without being able to say exactly why they mattered yet.

A ground crew was already towing the aircraft toward the launch area.

"They'll take her out to the pad," Garner told him.

Once outside, Delaney walked around the aircraft, taking it all in. "She's beautiful, in kind of a menacing way."

Garner just smiled. "Wait till you see what she can actually do."

Ten minutes later, rotors still folded, Pandora sat out on the tarmac. The sun was just climbing over the mountains, painting shades of copper and gold across the peaks. Delaney followed Garner up the ladder on the starboard side and into the cockpit.

Inside, the layout looked normal for a V-22 at first. But there was very little that was standard about the instrument panel. Mark Delaney slid into the right seat and stared at the extra screens and controls.

"This isn't your average bird," Garner said, buckling in. "Standard glass cockpit, fly-by-wire controls." He tapped a display. "Here's something special: terrain-following radar. Let's us skim the ground day or night, in any weather. They call it TF/TA."

A strange icon popped up on the screen as he flicked a switch.

"What's that?" Delaney asked, nodding toward the display.

"VEIL Gen 1. Variable Electronic Invisibility Layer," Garner said. "It scatters and deflects incoming radar. With the special paint, we're pretty much transparent to most radar out there. The Gen 2 system we'll eventually fly is more sophisticated, but this one does the job."

Delaney barely had time to process that when Garner pointed to another panel.

"This is the GAD. Gravimetric Anomaly Detector."

"A gravity wave sensor? I thought those were just for astrophysics, black holes, and stuff."

"Used to be just theory," Garner said. "Now it's real. We tuned it to pick up local gravitational anomalies. I did a lot of reading on the physics when they sent me the assignment brief."

Delaney stared at the display, shaking his head slowly. "I didn't think we were anywhere close to miniaturizing this kind of tech. LIGO uses kilometer-scale baselines. This shouldn't be possible in a cockpit."

"It wasn't," Garner said quietly. "Until it was."

Delaney looked at the display for a moment. He had spent four years in network defense, understanding systems by finding their limits. This one had no limits he could identify from the seat, which was either impressive or a sign that he didn't yet know enough to find them. Probably both.

More displays lit up as Garner ran through the MSSA. The Multi-Spectral Sensor Array swept the entire area, checking every spectrum for anything unusual.

"So, mapping atmospheric energy," Delaney guessed.

"Mapping sources of atmospheric energy," Garner corrected him. "Stuff that doesn't match known weather, power grids, or normal comms traffic. Unusual things. The things we're here to find."

The lieutenant leaned back, eying the unfamiliar configuration in front of him. The VEIL for stealth, the GAD and MSSA for tracking; definitely not your standard gear for combat or rescue. It didn't add up.

He paused, the smile fading. "Wait. You're serious. This is actually... we're actually..." He looked from Garner to the instrument panel and back. Then it hit him, and he let out a short laugh, turning to the captain. "You know, if I didn't know better, I'd say this whole setup's built for tracking something not from around here."

Garner didn't flinch. "We're here to gather data: to observe, identify, flag anything that might be a risk to national security. The sensors? They're tuned for ... let's just say, not everything you hear in the mess hall is pure fiction."

Delaney exhaled, taking in the cockpit's details. Now the name made sense. He gave a crooked, slightly nervous grin. "So that's why it's called Pandora. Not just a callsign, it's more like a box full of surprises. When do we get to see what it can do?"

"Right now," Garner said, and handed him a clipboard. "Preflight checklist."

Delaney had run checklists in Ospreys before. This one was longer. Some items he recognized; others had no equivalent in any aircraft he had trained on. He called them out anyway, and Garner confirmed each one without explanation, and by the time they reached the engine start sequence Delaney had decided that understanding would have to come later. For now he would fly the machine and learn what the items meant afterward.

The turbines spooled up, the proprotors unfolded, and the cockpit filled with a vibration that felt less like machinery and more like something alive deciding to move. A voice came through the headset, a little crackly. "Pandora, you're cleared for departure. Winds light and variable."

Garner eased up the collective, and Pandora lifted smoothly. At fifty feet, he pushed the nose forward; the aircraft climbed into the desert sky.

"Keep an eye on the nacelle transition," Garner said. "It's all automated, but the aircraft is making a decision about which machine it wants to be, and if you're fighting it instead of flying with it, she'll let you know."

The nacelles swung forward. The aircraft did not so much change modes as argue briefly with itself about whether to, and Delaney felt the disagreement through the stick before the airspeed sorted it out. At eighty knots the ride smoothed and Pandora became an airplane, a fast and responsive one, and he understood immediately why Garner flew her the way he did.

At five thousand feet over the desert, Garner released the controls. "Your airplane."

Delaney flew her through a left bank, a right bank, a climbing turn that tested the power margins and found them generous. She was heavy and precise and she did not forgive imprecision, which was the same thing Garner was, and Delaney suspected that was not an accident.

"Bring her back to helicopter mode," Garner said.

The return transition was harder than the first. Delaney bled the speed too quickly and felt the airframe shudder through a range it did not enjoy, and made three corrections where one smooth input would have done it. He got her into the hover eventually, two thousand feet up, the desert hanging below the chin windows.

"Again," Garner said.

They did it four more times. By the fourth, Delaney was making one correction instead of three.

He set her down on the tarmac and ran the shutdown sequence without being prompted. The rotors spun down. In the sudden quiet, Garner sat back.

"Not bad," he said.

They climbed out and walked around the plane. The lieutenant stopped at the nacelles, studying the intricate rotation mechanism. He checked the landing gear, tail, and the sensor pods along the fuselage.

"These sensors," he said, running his hand along one. "They aren't standard issue."

"Very little about Pandora is standard," Garner told him. "The MSSA gives us tools most pilots can only dream about. Thermal imaging, electromagnetic spectrum analysis, all on one display. The GAD is even more specialized. You just flew one of maybe three planes in the world with gravimetric sensors."

Delaney stepped back, taking in the black, angular shape of Pandora, bristling with tech that didn't belong in the world he knew.

"So what are we really hunting, Captain?"

Garner's face turned serious. "Things most people call myths. Objects that don't obey the laws of physics. And sometimes, we hunt the people chasing them."

Delaney nodded, taking it all in.

"When do we get our first mission?"

Garner said nothing. He crouched beside the port nacelle and ran his hand along the leading edge where the rotor housing met the fuselage skin, feeling for the slight warmth still radiating from the flight. He straightened, scanned the length of the aircraft once, then headed for the hangar door without looking back.

Delaney stayed where he was for a moment. In the hard light of the overhead floods, Pandora's black skin absorbed everything and gave nothing back. He thought about the sensors beneath it, the GAD reading gravity, the MSSA mapping things that had no business being in the sky.

Chapter Five

The Silent Visitor

Somewhere in the Nevada desert, soldiers with automatic weapons converged on wreckage in the sand, while the dust from their Humvees was still settling across the landscape. Their target was a saucer-shaped object with a smooth surface, reflecting the harsh desert sun.

"The perimeter is secured, General," shouted a colonel over the sound of Humvees and transport trucks.

Jonathan Briggs, a two-star U.S. Army general, acknowledged the report. "Advance with caution," he commanded. He was built square, with a jaw like a fist and the expression of a man who had stopped tolerating surprises years ago.

A shape broke the ridgeline: the unmistakable silhouette of a V-22, tilt-rotors already angled down as it dropped toward the desert floor.

"Aircraft approaching, General," an officer shouted.

The general turned his attention to an aircraft bearing no military insignia or corporate markings.

The landing gear of the Osprey had barely touched down as the side crew door opened. A figure emerged, dressed in a black environmental suit, and approached the general's command post, in defiance of the soldiers now training their weapons. Soldiers exchanged wary looks, shifting rifles uneasily. No one had expected a V-22 to break into restricted airspace without warning.

"Who the hell are you?" Briggs stormed forward and demanded as a woman approached. "This is a restricted military zone!"

"I am Director Kaela Renn," she said. "This incident is now under our jurisdiction. You will stand down your forces and withdraw to a five-mile perimeter."

Briggs laughed, but there was no humor in his voice. "On whose authority? This is a U.S. military operation, and my men are not moving. You may assist under my command structure. Is that clear?"

Renn raised a device resembling a wristwatch and pressed a button: "Inform the General of the status." A muffled sound from the device indicated a response.

A radioman approached the general with a radio. The general grabbed the handset.

"This is General Briggs." He had heard that voice before; you did not argue with that office.

The general listened, then handed back the handset with a single nod.

The general stiffened. Around him, his men watched, waiting for orders, hands still on their weapons.

Briggs's jaw worked as he stared at the radio. Finally, he nodded once, his voice tight.

"All units, fall back," he said, the words clipped and bitter. "Five-mile perimeter. Now."

The Pandora crew joined Director Renn.

Lieutenant Delaney stared at the alien craft. As soon as the others were out of hearing range, he asked, "Did I just see what I think I saw?"

The director smiled. "Welcome to your first Close Encounter."

"Now what?" he asked, glancing at Captain Garner.

The director crossed her arms.

"We wait," she said simply as she looked to the sky.

Garner said nothing. He stayed where he was.

High overhead, a shadow appeared without a sound, materializing into a cigar shape against the sky until it hovered above the downed saucer. The mother-ship held its position, massive and silent, two hundred feet of it blocking the stars above the site. It was waiting, not acting.

Delaney's training screamed to reach for a camera he wasn't allowed to carry.

"They're not taking it," Garner said quietly.

"Not yet," Renn said. "Their pilot is still aboard."

She crossed toward the alien craft at a steady pace. Garner returned to the aircraft. Delaney tracked him with one eye and kept the other on the MSSA display, which showed the positions of every military vehicle in the area. The perimeter had held since Briggs pulled his units back. Low-level logistics traffic on the main command channel. Nothing directed at the site.

Then the pattern changed.

Three rapid transmissions on a secondary net, not the main command channel. A unit frequency, the kind a squad used when it didn't want the colonel to hear. Delaney pulled the feed and processed it in under ten seconds.

Someone on the northeast side of the perimeter had just been told to move.

"We have a problem," he said, keeping his voice level. "Radio spike on a secondary net. One vehicle, northeast side. It hasn't stopped moving."

Through the windscreen he could already see the dust rising beyond the tree line.

He could try jamming the frequency. A soft block would buy thirty seconds, maybe less, before they switched channels. Out near the alien craft, Renn had reached the hull. The pilot was still inside. Thirty seconds was not going to be enough.

He ran the jam anyway. He bought what he could and passed the rest of the problem to Garner.

"Russ. Humvee at your two o'clock. Moving toward the site."

Garner was already at the cockpit door.

A shape appeared at the torn opening in the saucer's hull. The being moved carefully at first, pausing in the threshold and taking in the desert and the aircraft beyond. Then it stepped into the sunlight. Barely four feet tall, elongated all the same, with limbs and skull out of proportion to its compact frame, pale skin faintly iridescent in the morning light. Large black eyes moved across the scene without blinking. One arm was held close at an awkward angle, injured in whatever had brought the saucer down. It stepped toward Renn with careful, deliberate steps.

The Humvee broke clear of the brush two hundred yards out, angling hard across the desert floor. The path it was taking would cut directly in front of the alien before Renn could guide it back to Pandora.

Garner climbed into the left seat and pulled the door.

He brought the port engine up two hundred RPM. Not a liftoff. Not even a hover. Just enough rotor power to put a moving wall of wind between the aircraft and the Humvee. He rotated Pandora ten degrees on its axis and pushed the power up another notch.

The rotor wash hit the desert floor in a sheet of churned dust and grit. Garner held the power exactly where he needed it. Too much and the alien went over; too little and the vehicle kept coming. He could feel the tradeoff through the collective, the same narrow band he had worked in over the Syrian border: the gap between what the manual said and what the aircraft could actually do.

He did not close his eyes or second guess. He held the trim and watched.

The Humvee slewed left, but the driver corrected. Then the rotor wash caught the high side of the vehicle and pushed again. The Humvee came to a stop forty yards short of where it needed to be.

Renn kept moving. She did not look back. She had read the situation from the change in the wind and trusted Garner to close it.

Delaney killed the jam. The secondary frequency lit back up at once; the driver's voice was sharp and confused.

They had maybe fifteen seconds. The count was ten. Then eight. Renn hadn't moved.

"Ramp," Garner said.

Delaney operated the hydraulic controls, and the rear ramp lowered to the ground.

As Captain Garner climbed fully into the left seat, Delaney stared at the camera feed from the rear cabin. What he saw defied everything he had expected.

Up close, on the camera feed, the scale of it hit differently. Garner's overhead lights caught the injured arm first, braced against the torso at an angle that needed no medical training to read. A flat, non-color somewhere between gunmetal and deep water, the suit absorbed the cabin light rather than reflecting it, shifting subtly as the being moved, as if the fabric were making a continuous small adjustment. Narrow face, skull higher than a human skull had any reason to be, and across the cheekbones a faint subsurface quality, as though the fluorescence came from somewhere inside rather than landing on the surface. Three-fingered hands stayed still. Those black eyes moved across the interior in a single slow sweep, methodical, registering nothing Delaney could read as recognition or fear. Whatever it was taking in, it was filing, not reacting.

As the ramp rose and the desert light narrowed to a line and then disappeared, the Gray went very still, the black eyes moving once across the sealed interior and then fixing on Renn.

Garner pressed the intercom button for the rear cabin. "What's our next step?"

The tall being was startled at the sound, then looked to Director Renn and visibly relaxed.

Renn turned toward the camera. "We wait for the ship to come to us. Hold position."

"Copy," Garner replied.

The desert outside was still. The Humvee had not moved again. Through the camera feed, Delaney watched the dust around it settle. Whoever had given that driver his orders had apparently thought better of explaining himself to Briggs.

The mother ship descended.

It came down slow and deliberate, the cigar shape growing until its shadow covered Pandora and the open ground around it. A portal opened in its side and a platform extended toward the desert floor. The alien stood from its seat in the rear cabin and moved toward the ramp.

Renn opened it. Warm desert air rolled in. The alien paused at the threshold for a moment, its long fingers brushing Renn's arm. A silent exchange passed between them. Then it walked down the ramp and crossed the open ground to the waiting platform.

The platform retracted. The portal closed.

The mother ship turned its attention to the wrecked saucer. Slowly, the giant vessel elevated the craft until it hung as if suspended by an unseen force. It rose and tilted once as the hold found its balance, then straightened and vanished.

The director exhaled. "That's our part done," she said quietly as she raised her hand and pointed, and the crew headed back to the cockpit.

Back aboard the Osprey, the pilots settled in. Director Renn took a position in the jump seat at the rear of the cockpit while Garner and Delaney began the pre-flight checklist.

"Avionics check complete, warning panel clear." Captain Garner marked each item on a small clipboard.

"Throttle idle, flaps up, nacelles forward, hydraulic check, rotors engaged, flight controls responsive, landing gear up, check."

Delaney confirmed each step.

Outside, the desert dust blown by the powerful propellers completely blocked the view from the cockpit.

"Rotor RPM nominal, throttle advance."

Captain Garner took the controls as the plane lifted off.

Delaney turned toward the director and pressed the intercom button on his headset control.

"Director," he said, his voice cutting into the steady engine hum. "Permission to speak freely?"

"This is your first mission on the E-Team. I'm sure you have many questions, so go ahead."

"OK, what was the army going to do with that thing?" Delaney asked.

"Probably load it onto a flatbed and try to sneak it onto a base somewhere, then hand it over to some contractor, like they've done with the others. Years ago, one unit thought they could chop up a flying saucer with blowtorches. As you might imagine, it didn't work."

"So how did the spaceship crash?"

"Because it was shot down with a Targeted Energy Beam," the director answered.

"Wouldn't the aliens have superior weapons? Why didn't they use them?"

Garner finally spoke, his voice measured and even. "What she's saying is, Lieutenant, if they responded by burning through an Army cordon with tech no one's supposed to know exists, then the game's over. Our mission is to maintain the balance."

Director Renn added, "As you saw, the larger ships can become invisible. That's how they can avoid direct conflict."

"So whose side are we on? Where does Mogul fit in?" Delaney asked.

"Project Mogul," Renn corrected. "1947. You know about the so-called Roswell crash? Everyone was told it was a balloon project. High-altitude acoustic sensors to spy on Soviet nukes. That was the cover. The truth is, Mogul became the first formal liaison program. Only back then, nobody outside the circle knew what they were looking at. So they let them believe in little green men, in abductions, in tinfoil hats. The clutter kept the truth hidden in plain sight."

"And today? What was in that wreck?"

Renn's stern expression didn't change. "One of their own. Injured. Trapped. The saucer was expendable. The occupant wasn't. That's why we're here. To keep people like General Briggs from carting it off to Lockheed or Raytheon and turning it into a weapons program and doing experiments on any survivors. Mogul doesn't answer to contractors. We answer to a higher authority, above top secret."

"Above the Pentagon? Is that what they call the 'deep state'?"

Renn's expression did not change. But she did not correct him either.

He shifted gears. "They've been here a long time. Why Earth?"

"Monatomic gold or ORME gold," Captain Garner said. "It's apparently key to their anti-gravity propulsion systems. The way it naturally forms here, with its crystal structure and diamagnetic properties, is in a form they need."

Delaney was confused. "So why are they so interested in our nuclear bases? I heard they took over the launch controls at a Russian base. They even messed with the Minuteman nukes at Malmstrom."

Renn chimed in, "Think of it this way: if they allow us to blow up this planet, there goes their source of raw materials. Maybe they like to remind us of what they can do."

Captain Garner added, "They're operating on a long game, Lieutenant. Engagement costs them more than retreat."

"So why does the government, the part we work for, keep the population in the dark?" Delaney asked.

Renn smiled. "The answer to that question is complicated, and will need to wait for another day."

The Osprey's shadow raced below, a swift, dark shape gliding over the arid earth. To the north, the stark white expanse of Groom Lake, a dry salt flat, glared under the sun. As the aircraft banked south, the land rose into the barren brown folds of the Pintwater Range, and sharp ridges cast deep shadows across canyons littered with boulders.

Delaney and Captain Garner turned their attention to the landing.

***

It was well after dark when they landed. Director Renn climbed down and headed inside. Aboard Pandora, Garner and Delaney worked through the landing checklist. As they checked off the last item, they climbed out of the aircraft.

The floodlights threw long shadows across the ground as Garner signaled to the ground crew, waiting to tow the aircraft inside the hangar.

As they walked toward the base away from the aircraft, Mark tapped on Russ's shoulder and the two stopped.

"Can you fill me in on something?" Delaney asked. "Who are these creatures and where do they come from?"

Captain Garner smiled. "I wondered when you would ask about that. When I was in the military, there were a lot of things we saw, but didn't talk about. We knew better. We came to accept that there are things in the sky." He adjusted the strap on his gear bag. "What we encountered today are the Grays. The common perception is that they originated in the Zeta Reticuli star system. I've come to understand they may be the most ancient visitors."

"Before today I assumed it was all just legend and rumors."

"When you were recruited for this program, what were you expecting?"

The tow disappeared into the hangar, and the huge, camouflaged door closed, leaving the two men alone in the night air.

Mark looked at the ground, then looked up and smiled. "I assumed this was part of some kind of CIA black ops." He raised his hand in a helpless gesture. "Nothing like any of this."

"The Grays are not the only species we'll be meeting. There's another species we'll likely encounter, what the reports call Nordics. Human-sized, blond, blue-eyed. They blend in almost perfectly. Separate species from Tall Whites entirely."

"Where are they from?" Mark asked.

Captain Garner explained, "It is said they are from the Pleiades star cluster, what astronomers call the Seven Sisters. The interesting thing is that they might have a lifespan as long as eight hundred years."

"How does that work?"

"I don't know how true they are, but some classified reports claim they develop in stages. The first phase can last as long as sixty years, when they are relatively human-sized, maybe five or six feet tall, blond, blue-eyed. They could walk through any European city without a second glance."

"Are there others?" Mark asked.

"Maybe, maybe not," Russ replied with a mysterious smile.

"So, what's this all about?" Delaney was growing impatient.

"You'll hear stories, some true, some not, about agreements with governments, exchanges of technology, some official, some not official. There are forces at work, forces that could disrupt the delicate balance. That's the reason behind Project Mogul, to maintain that balance. That's what our job is about."

With that, Captain Garner smiled and turned to open the crew door as the pair entered the S-3 facility.

Chapter Six

The Facts of Life

Back at the base, Lieutenant Mark Delaney was uncharacteristically quiet as he and Russ Garner walked around the Pandora. They each carried an iFly EFB Aviation tablet. Captain Garner filled out the ForeFlight log, while Delaney handled the aircraft's technical log records.

With the walk-around inspection tasks completed, they headed to the Ready Room while the ground crew towed Pandora into the hangar. Russ announced he was heading for the mess kitchen and offered to bring back coffee. Delaney declined the offer.

On returning with his coffee, Captain Garner studied Mark's face.

"You're wound up. Something on your mind, Rook?"

Mark hesitated, then looked up. "Just sorting things out in my mind, I guess, Captain."

"In what way?" Garner responded. "By the way, we're not on the flight deck. You can call me Russ."

Mark nodded and continued. "There are thousands of UAP reports, and the public eats it up. Some guy on YouTube claimed he was on board a flying saucer and saw stars streaming by the windows. Stars are billions of miles away. They don't fly by like trees on a highway, no matter how fast the ship is going. It's physics."

Russ chimed in, "I like the one where one witness said the inside of a UFO smelled like cinnamon."

Mark chuckled. "Right. Or the woman who saw aliens wearing Rolex watches. Then there was that alien autopsy. It turned out to be lamb bones." He rubbed his face. "The government covers up genuine cases, the public invents impossible ones, and military contractors are right there to make a buck in the middle of it all. Meanwhile, we can't tell anyone which is which."

"And now anyone with a laptop and a free afternoon can generate footage that fools a Senate subcommittee," Russ added. "We spent three days last month tracing a viral video back to a graphics student in Tempe."

"So where does it end?"

Russ took a last sip of his coffee, then set the empty cup on the desk. "It doesn't end; that's the point."

Mark leaned forward, elbows on his knees. "Then what are we doing? Just plugging holes in a dam that's already cracked?"

Russ shook his head. "We're not plugging holes. We're relieving the pressure, one leak at a time."

Mark was quiet for a moment. "With thousands of UFO reports, they're not exactly keeping a low profile. What are they doing?"

"My guess? Observation. Monitoring." Russ shrugged. "As we've seen, they're not subtle about it."

Mark glanced toward the hangar where the Pandora was being secured.

"I used to think this job was about solving a problem. Someone above the Joint Chiefs hands us the problem and expects us to contain it."

Mark nodded slowly. "And the public?"

"They get stories. A few might be real, but most are not." Russ spoke with a flat, level tone. "Doesn't matter. The noise keeps them busy. Keeps the scary ones buried."

Mark stood and walked to the door, watching the maintenance crew work. "Makes you wonder where they come from. They can't be commuting from some distant galaxy."

"Probably not. I don't have a good answer for that. Neither did any of the briefings I've read."

"So what happens when containment fails?"

Russ met his eyes. "We do what we were hired to do. Isolate, intercept, and if necessary, erase the evidence. Quietly. Cleanly."

Mark didn't respond right away. "And if that's not enough?"

Russ picked up his empty coffee cup and gestured to illustrate his point as he headed toward the kitchen. "Then we adapt. That's the job. Not to solve it, just to stay ahead of it where we can."

"But we can't even be sure what's real." Russ turned back from the door as Mark continued. "All those stories about agreements between aliens and governments, going back to the fifties. Which aliens? Which governments? Is any of it real?"

"You mean the Eisenhower story? Edwards Air Force Base?" Russ shook his head. "Why would any president agree to let aliens abduct people in exchange for technology? And he wouldn't have had the authority anyway. Treaties go through Congress."

"So it's fake?"

"Probably. But who knows?" Russ absently tapped his fingers on the empty cup. "That was years ago. If it were real, how much research would they need by now?"

Mark crossed his arms. "Another thing. Why do so many of their ships crash?"

Russ thought for a moment. "There's an old theory about Roswell, that a high-powered radar pulse interfered with the propulsion system. The military was testing the radar at White Sands, Alamogordo, and other sites across New Mexico back then."

"Is that what really happened?"

Russ paused. "Maybe. Some reports said the radar at Walker Field picked up a second ship that escaped."

Mark nodded slowly. "How many years between then and now? That's a lot of crashes."

Russ smiled. "And they would have developed a defense by now."

"Which brings me to Nevada." Mark looked up. "Briggs was right there when that ship went down. Then someone at the Pentagon calls him and suddenly he's backing off like he knows he shouldn't be there. Did he shoot it down?"

"Someone did," Russ replied. "Prometheus Applied Sciences. They're the ones shooting down alien craft to harvest technology. That's the reason this program exists."

"What if they're not just recovering crashes?" Mark leaned against the doorframe. "What if they're creating them, then reverse-engineering the tech to build weapons?"

Russ was quiet. "That would make the company very valuable. And very dangerous."

"And a Special Operations general shows up right when one goes down. That's not coincidence." Mark's eyes narrowed. "Does Briggs know something?"

"Maybe. But he gave up too easily when he got that call. Like he knew he didn't have the authority to be there." Russ met his gaze. "Like maybe he had a guilty conscience."

"Could Briggs be connected with Prometheus?"

"Could be involved. Could be nothing." Russ's tone was carefully neutral. "Reverse-engineered tech, weaponized. Briggs showing up right when things go wrong. It's a pattern, but patterns don't prove anything."

Mark glanced toward the door again, making sure they were alone. "What about Alaska? Earlier this year, those fighter jets scrambling over the Yukon shot down something that definitely wasn't a weather balloon, and nobody's explained it since."

"I noticed that too."

"So who decides what missions we get?" He glanced toward the closed door of the director's office. "Renn won't say, but it's got to be someone at the Pentagon."

Russ was quiet.

"Can't answer or won't answer?"

"Either way."

Mark changed direction. “I’ve got theories about how they make those ninety-degree turns at speed.”

Russ looked intrigued. “I’d like to hear that theory.”

“Anti-gravity propulsion. We get readings on the Gravimetric Anomaly Detector, right? If you control gravity, you could control mass and weight. No mass means no inertia. No inertia means no restrictions on turns.”

Russ smiled slowly. “I’ve wondered about that, but I never made that connection.” He set down his cup again.

They sat in silence for a moment, mechanical sounds from the hangar filtering through the walls.

“You know what bothers me most?” Mark said finally. “We’re out here flying into the unknown, and we don’t even know who we’re working for.”

Garner glanced toward the hangar where the ground crew was still working, then back at Delaney. “We got a call, we responded, and an eight-foot alien made it home tonight. I’m going to focus on that part.”

Mark looked at him, then nodded slowly.

The door to Renn’s office opened, and she walked toward them. Had she heard their discussion?

“I sense you have some questions about our mission here.”

Garner decided against a second cup of coffee and returned to his seat at the table.

“The E-Team exists for one reason,” Renn said. “To keep our own government from turning a diplomatic problem into an extinction-level event. Every overt appearance has the potential to destabilize markets, alliances, even religions. One open landing and half the world assumes the other half has already made a deal.” She folded her arms. “The visitors have learned that humanity is not afraid of the unknown. We’re afraid of each other gaining an advantage from it.”

“If they’re hiding, they’re not very good at it,” Mark inserted.

Renn met his eyes. “They’re good enough.”

"They're visible enough to be undeniable and ambiguous enough to be unprovable," she said. "That gap is the only thing keeping someone's hand off a trigger right now."

She glanced around the table. "Our job is to make sure it stays that way."

Outside, the ground crew rolled the hangar doors shut with a metallic boom that echoed through the Ready Room.

Chapter Seven

The Rescue

Later that week, Lieutenant Delaney returned from a training flight to find Director Renn in the Ready Room studying a map on the big screen.

"Good. You're back," she said. "I have a set of coordinates for you."

"Okay, I'll file a flight plan ..." he replied.

"Not this time." She handed him a note with the coordinates.

Delaney paused, expecting a reason, but the director waved him off.

"Let me know when the plane is ready so I can join you."

Delaney pulled the door open and almost walked into Captain Garner coming down the corridor.

"Don't get too relaxed," Delaney said, holding up the note. "I'll top off the fuel and set the navigation. Renn's waiting inside."

Garner stepped into the Ready Room. Renn was at the screen, the coordinates already marked.

"We can be ready when you are," Garner said. "No flight plan?"

"No need. Short hop, low altitude, all within range. We're ghosts on this one."

Garner followed Renn out to Pandora.

"Navigation's set," Delaney reported as the other two climbed on board. Renn strapped into the jump seat behind the pilots.

Captain Garner turned to Renn and asked, "Talk to me. What's the mission?"

"A rescue. An F-16 collided with an alien craft. No one is calling it hostile. The Air Force is treating it as an in-flight collision during a training exercise. Whatever caused it, the craft came down intact enough to have a survivor."

"The military has a perimeter. How do we extract an alien pilot out from under their noses without triggering a firefight?"

"The military already rescued their pilot. They won't be back until they figure out how to get a truck in to recover the wreckage."

Delaney stopped the preflight checklist, turning to stare at the director. "Rescue who, then?"

"We need to get the other pilot out of there before they come back."

Captain Garner tightened his grip on the clipboard. "Extraction and evasion, then. We're running a jailbreak."

Renn's response was stern. "The military will cover up the collision, they always do. But if a mother ship shows up to retrieve their pilot, there's no story that explains that. That's where we come in. Let's go."

Lieutenant Delaney probably had a lot of questions on his mind, but he kept them to himself while they completed the takeoff checklist.

"Ready?" Captain Garner asked.

"Roger," Delaney answered.

Captain Garner then shouted, "Clear!" and Pandora's twin Rolls-Royce AE 1107C turboshaft engines roared to life.

The target location was a desolate spot in the New Mexico desert, only a few hundred miles away. At just below 300 miles an hour, Pandora covered the distance quickly, remaining below radar as it followed the terrain, one of Pandora's special capabilities.

As they approached the area, Director Renn pointed to an object among the rocks a short distance ahead. "That's our target."

The target was a disc-shaped object, maybe thirty feet across, its surface a flat silver-white with no visible seams or markings.

Delaney leaned forward to view the object. "I've seen the classified imagery. Nothing prepared me for seeing one in the field."

Captain Garner set Pandora into a hover one hundred yards out, far enough that the rotor wash wouldn't disturb the wreckage.

"Your airplane," he commanded as he transferred control to his copilot. Turning to Director Renn, he asked, "What's our next step?"

"We recover a non-human entity. Can we find a suitable place to land?"

Garner pointed to a spot a short distance away. Delaney nodded and set the controls to lower the aircraft.

As the plane settled onto the desert floor, the engines came to a slow idle, and the dust settled.

The damage to the alien craft from the collision was obvious. A gaping hole in one side made the disc look more like a cracked plate.

"You stay with the plane while we size up the situation."

Garner opened the cockpit door, and he and the director climbed down.

Renn paused as they approached the alien craft.

Garner noted her expression. "Do you have a headache?" he asked. Renn waved off the question, her expression distant with concentration. "It's okay."

A tall, nonhuman figure appeared at the opening in the spacecraft. The being was apprehensive at first, but then seemed reassured and moved into the desert sunlight. Renn turned, and the visitor followed her to the aircraft.

Captain Garner watched, stunned by what he was seeing. The cockpit door was still open as they approached. He called back to Delaney: "Lower the ramp. We have a passenger."

Lieutenant Delaney operated the hydraulic controls, and the rear ramp slowly lowered to the ground, allowing Director Renn and their new passenger to board.

As Captain Garner climbed into the left seat, Delaney pulled up the rear cabin feed out of habit. He had seen a Gray stand in this aircraft's rotor wash. He thought that had prepared him for something. Looking at the camera now, he understood it had prepared him for nothing.

The visitor had to stoop significantly to enter; its towering frame making the Osprey's interior feel suddenly cramped. Its movements were liquid and careful, as if it were acutely aware of the fragility of the human machinery around it. It had to fold itself to clear the cabin roof, and even stooped, it filled the frame of the camera in a way the Gray never had. Where the Gray had been compact and contained, this being was architecture, all vertical lines and controlled length, built for a scale the aircraft was never designed to accommodate. The skin carried no shimmer, no iridescence, just a flat chalk-white that the cabin lights landed on without softening. The face was angular where the Gray's had been narrow, the cheekbones broader, the jaw carrying more structure. And the eyes were wrong in a completely different way than the Gray's had been: not black, not absorbing, but blue, vivid and specific, the kind of blue that registered as deliberate rather than biological, as if whatever was behind them had chosen to be seen.

The visitor wore what appeared to be a form-fitting suit in a color Delaney couldn't quite identify, somewhere between silver and blue, with a slight iridescence that shifted as the being moved. One arm was held close to the torso at an awkward angle, likely injured in the collision.

As the ramp closed, the Tall White went still. Its head turned toward the sealed door, and then it did not move again, standing at full height in a cabin built for something considerably smaller, watching the interior the way something watches when it has decided to wait rather than act.

Garner pressed the intercom button for the rear cabin. "What's next?" he asked.

The tall being startled at the sound, eyes widening, then looking to Director Renn and visibly relaxing.

Director Renn pulled a note from her pocket. "We have rendezvous coordinates. Ready to copy?" she asked.

"Roger that," Delaney replied, still transfixed by the image on his screen.

Renn read out the numbers: "33.952189 degrees North by 105.331214 West."

Delaney read the numbers back. "Confirmed," the director replied, and the engines powered up for takeoff.

The designated location was in an area managed by the Bureau of Land Management outside of Corona, New Mexico. They settled in for a landing and shut off the engines. Through the rear cabin camera feed, Renn unstrapped from the jump seat and moved into the cabin.

Garner hit the switch. The ramp came down. He cracked his door and listened. Nothing. Just the tick of cooling metal and the wind off the high desert.

Then he watched Renn through the camera. She had her eyes closed.

Delaney had been watching the MSSA since the wheels touched down. The surrounding terrain read clean: no vehicles, no heat signatures, nothing at ground level. He let himself breathe.

Then the sweep caught something forty miles out and closing. Military fast-movers, a pair of them, tracking a search pattern that was going to bring them directly over the BLM site in about twelve minutes.

"We have company," he said. "Two contacts, four-zero miles. Search pattern. They're working the crash site area."

Garner looked at the display. "They came back fast."

"Faster than the director projected." Delaney pulled the transponder settings. "VEIL is active. They won't paint us on radar, but if they come in low enough for a visual pass we're sitting on flat ground in a white aircraft."

"Can we lift?"

Delaney turned in his seat toward the rear camera. Through the feed, he could see Renn in the cabin with the Tall White. She had one hand extended toward the being, not touching it, just close. Her eyes were still closed. The alien had pulled itself upright in the seat and was watching her with its large blue eyes.

"Not yet. She's got contact."

Garner checked the MSSA readout again. Eleven minutes. "If we're still on the ground when they come through their search corridor, we light up on optical before VEIL can do anything about it."

"I know," Delaney said.

They both looked at the camera feed.

***

In the rear cabin, Renn could feel the connection fraying.

The Tall White's mind had the quality she associated with its species: close to conversation, almost structured. But the injured arm was doing something she hadn't expected. Pain interrupted the channel in sharp bursts, the way a bad radio line cuts in and out in a storm. Every time she thought she had the contact stable, a spike of physical distress from the alien broke through and scattered it.

The being was frightened. Not of her. Of waiting.

The ship does not know where we are.

The thought arrived in fragments, not quite words. Renn steadied herself and pushed back through the channel, projecting as clearly as she could.

It will find you. I'm keeping you here until it does. Stay with me.

Another burst of pain from the injured arm. The contact slipped. Renn tightened her focus and pulled it back, which cost her more than she would have admitted to Garner.

The headache had moved behind her left eye. She had learned not to show it. The being was watching her with those vivid blue eyes, and she understood that if she looked distressed, it would try to stand, try to move. An eight-foot being with a broken arm and nowhere to go was a problem she did not need.

Stay with me.

The Tall White settled back a fraction.

Through the cockpit partition, she heard Delaney's voice. Not the words, just the tone. Something had changed outside.

***

"Eight minutes," Delaney said. "They're not deviating."

Garner kept his hands off the controls. Starting the engines would be the loudest thing that happened in this valley for a week. Even at idle they'd be audible from two miles, and two miles was nothing to a jet doing a low search pass.

"We hold," he said.

"And if they come in below five hundred feet?"

"We hold." Garner's voice did not change. "A cold aircraft on flat ground in low light looks like a lot of things. An aircraft that just started its engines looks like exactly one thing."

Delaney shut down every active emitter he could reach without killing the camera feeds. The MSSA went passive. The GAD dropped to standby. Pandora sat dark and silent on the desert floor.

Six minutes.

Delaney watched the camera feed. Renn had not moved. Her hand was still extended toward the alien, not quite touching. Whatever she was doing, it was costing her. He could see it in the set of her jaw.

Four minutes. The contacts were close enough now that he could read the flight profile. They were working a standard grid, parallel lines two miles apart, which meant their next pass was going to bring them directly overhead or within a quarter mile of it.

"They're going to see us if they come in at pattern altitude," he said.

"Then we hope they're at altitude," Garner replied. He did not look away from the windscreen.

The sound reached them before the aircraft did. A low, compressed thunder rolling down from the north, building as it came.

Two F-16s crossed the valley at twelve hundred feet, fast and straight, working their line. Neither aircraft dipped. Neither deviated. Their search pattern carried them two miles east of Pandora's position and on through the far ridgeline, the sound fading behind them like a receding wave.

Delaney let out a breath. "They're through."

"How long until the next pass?"

Delaney checked the track. "Eighteen minutes if they hold the grid."

"Then we need the ship inside eighteen minutes."

***

Garner noticed the director's expression shift first, the look she wore before contact, somewhere between a headache and fierce concentration.

He watched through the camera as the Tall White straightened in its seat and turned toward the ramp. Renn opened her eyes.

"It's coming," she said. Her voice was steady, but she kept one hand braced against the bulkhead.

A shape appeared high above, slowly descending through the wispy clouds. The shape grew larger. A disc-shaped craft, massive and dim, descended through the overcast clouds.

What appeared to be landing gear or pods extended as the craft came in for a landing fifty yards from the Pandora.

An opening appeared in the spacecraft.

Pandora's guest stood, unfolding to full height, towering over Director Renn even with the injured posture. The being moved with careful deliberation despite the injured arm and walked down the ramp toward the waiting spacecraft.

At the base of the ramp, the tall visitor paused and turned back. Through the camera, Delaney watched as the being's long fingers touched its chest, then extended toward Pandora in what could only be a gesture of gratitude. Then it turned and entered the spacecraft.

The craft hovered for a moment before rapidly rising into the clouds.

Director Renn strapped into a seat in the rear cabin. She took one slow breath before her voice came through the intercom. "Let's go home."

Through the rear camera, Delaney watched Renn reach up and press two fingers to her left temple, hold them there for a moment, then drop her hand and look out the window at nothing. She did not move again for the first forty minutes of the flight home. Garner saw it too. Neither of them said anything.

With the data entered into the navigation system and the flight plan filed, the Pandora took off and headed back to the base.

As they climbed to cruising altitude, Garner glanced at the camera feed. The rear cabin was empty, the ramp sealed.

He did not ask about the headache. She would tell him or she wouldn't. He had learned that much.

***

As they landed and powered down, the crew climbed down from the cockpit.

Delaney stopped Director Renn as she was heading back inside.

"This mission didn't come from headquarters, did it?"

Director Renn smiled but did not answer.

Hours later, Mark and Russ were relaxing in the Ready Room. The news channel was displayed on the big screen.

"Turn that up," Mark said as a picture of the downed jet appeared on the screen.

Russ reached for the TV remote.

They heard the news reporter say, "A fighter jet on a training flight experienced an engine failure and crashed in a remote area of the New Mexico desert. An Air Force HH-60 Pave Hawk from Holloman Air Force Base successfully rescued their pilot."

"And they hauled the thing off to the NSA Puzzle Palace, at Fort Meade, like they always do," Russ said. "I bet they wonder where the pilot went."

Mark was quiet for a moment, his mind replaying the experience. The extraordinarily tall being with chalk-white skin. And those eyes. The elongated proportions that seemed barely suited for Earth's gravity.

"Eight feet tall," he said quietly. "Maybe more. I've read about Tall Whites in the UFO reports, but seeing one ..." He shook his head. "Charles Hall's accounts from Indian Springs, an Air Force weather observer who claimed years of contact with them. I always wondered if they were real."

"They're real," Russ said. "Other pilots talked about them. Sightings during night ops, something tall moving at the edge of the flightline, gone before anyone could be sure. I never saw one myself, but you don't fly long enough without hearing the stories." He paused. "Stronger gravity than Earth, that's the theory. You can tell by how they move. Almost floating."

"The way the director communicated with it," Mark said. "She didn't speak. Neither did it."

"Telepathy," Russ said. "From what I've gathered, Tall Whites communicate primarily through direct mental contact. For them, spoken language is secondary."

Mark nodded slowly. "That's why she gets the headaches. When she's making contact."

"Probably." Russ set down his coffee. "Though I noticed today was harder than usual."

"The arm," Mark said. "The pain was breaking the channel. She had to keep pulling it back."

Russ was quiet for a moment. "She held it together until the ship arrived."

"She held it together while two F-16s were doing search passes overhead." Mark looked at his coffee. "That's not something they covered in flight school."

"Nothing about this is something they covered in flight school," Russ replied.

They sat in silence, watching the news anchor move on to the next story. Somewhere in Virginia, intelligence analysts were probably examining the recovered Tic Tac, running tests on materials they couldn't identify.

"You know what strikes me?" Mark said finally. "We just rescued an eight-foot-tall alien from a crashed spacecraft, returned it to a mother ship that can appear and disappear at will, sat cold on a desert floor while the Air Force searched for us overhead, and tomorrow we'll file a report that says we ran a routine systems test."

"Welcome to Project Mogul," Russ said with a slight smile. "Where the impossible becomes routine, and the routine is classified."

Mark leaned back in his chair. "Grays and Tall Whites. Makes you wonder how many others are out there."

"Probably more than we know," Russ replied. "And probably less than the conspiracy theorists claim. The truth is somewhere in between."

The news continued playing, but neither man was really watching anymore. They were both thinking about the tall being they'd rescued. About the casual way Director Renn had held the contact open for twenty minutes with a headache pushing behind her eye and military aircraft cutting through the valley overhead.

And about how their job was to stand in the middle of it all, managing the chaos, keeping the peace, and making sure that humanity's steps into a larger universe didn't end in catastrophe.

"Think we'll see more of them?" Mark asked. "The Tall Whites?"

"Probably," Russ said. "If they've been visiting Nevada for as long as the reports suggest, they're not going anywhere."

Mark nodded. That was the reality of Project Mogul. They weren't solving the alien question. They were managing it. One mission at a time, one species at a time, one impossible situation at a time.

Chapter Eight

Pandora 2

At morning chow, Director Renn's eyes telegraphed bad news before she spoke.

"I'm afraid, effective immediately, all Osprey flights are restricted to a thirty-minute radius. No extended flights, no over water legs beyond that window."

"Why would they do that?" Lieutenant Delaney asked.

"There's a problem with the propeller gearbox," the director answered. "There have been several fatal crashes. They don't want to take any chances until they find a fix."

Renn nodded grimly. "It's the clutch, Captain," she explained. "When the clutch slips, it can suddenly re-engage with a shock load that tears through the drive train. Basically, it strips the gears."

"If they can't find a solid fix, I suspect they could be phasing out the Osprey," Garner said, peering at Delaney over the rim of his mug.

Delaney froze, the coffee halfway to his lips. "Phasing out? What does that mean for the Project? Are we being shut down?" He looked to the director for an answer.

Delaney set his cup down, shaking his head. "We finally get good at something, and they ground the only tool that works."

"Not yet," she said, looking at her watch. "Pack your duffle bags and meet me outside the hangar door at zero-seven-thirty. Expect to be on tour for thirty days."

At 0730, outside the compound, the same unmarked white bus was waiting for the pilots, like a ghost from their first arrival. The silent ride back to the Area 51 complex was a familiar, though disappointing, experience.

Two men in flight suits greeted them in an isolated hangar instead of a briefing room.

"Captain, Lieutenant." One of them stepped forward with the unhurried confidence of someone who had forgotten more about tilt-rotor aircraft than most pilots would ever learn. "Mason. This is Jacobs." He didn't offer a rank or a branch, which told Garner everything he needed to know about the clearance level of the program they were running. Jacobs was younger, quieter, and carried a tablet he hadn't looked up from since they walked in.

"Instructors for what?" Delaney asked.

Mason didn't answer. He turned toward the back of the hangar. "Come see."

They walked to the back of the hangar. Outside on the tarmac was an unfamiliar tilt-rotor aircraft, slightly smaller and more angular than the Osprey. The tilt-rotors rose from stationary engines fixed to the wings.

"Gentlemen, meet the Bell V-280 Valor," Jacobs said. "This is your new bird."

Delaney circled the plane, noting the details. It had wide side doors. In the cockpit were four seats, compared to the Osprey's two, plus that cramped jump seat Renn used.

Delaney and Garner climbed into the rear of the cockpit. It had a distinctive smell of fresh paint. Mason leaned in to point out the updated glass cockpit. Where the display in the Osprey was merely functional, the V-280 had large, reconfigurable displays.

"The airframe is carbon fiber, so she's lighter and more compact," Jacobs explained. "The V-280 is a real step forward from the Osprey. Instead of the whole nacelle rotating like on the V-22, the engines stay fixed and just the rotors tilt. That means fewer moving parts to maintain and better reliability when you need it. The fly-by-wire system has triple redundancy built in, and you'll notice the difference right away in the hover and low-speed handling, much more responsive than what you're used to."

"How about a test ride?" Mason asked. Noting agreement, he climbed into the left seat, followed close behind by Jacobs, who took the right seat.

Captain Garner and Delaney took the rear two seats and strapped in.

The pilot started the engines and radioed the tower for taxiway clearance to the helicopter pad. The takeoff was smooth. Once in the air, the conversion from helicopter to airplane mode was seamless. During the hour-long flight, the pilots put the aircraft through its paces, demonstrating the superior speed over that of the Osprey.

Back on the ground, Mason laid out the plan.

"As rated V-22 pilots, the pipeline for you two is four weeks. We're on a temporary assignment from Marine Corps Air Station New River in Jacksonville, North Carolina. When we sign off on your training, you'll be taking this aircraft to your base. You start tomorrow morning. If there are no questions, Jacobs here will direct you to your temporary quarters."

Week one was ground school. Mason ran it with the efficiency of someone who had given the same material a hundred times and still believed every word of it. The fixed-engine design, the digital backbone, the modular integration architecture: each system connected to the next in a chain that Delaney found himself following with genuine interest, which surprised him. He had come up through networks and code. He had not expected aircraft systems to feel familiar.

On the third day he said so, spreading the schematic across the table. "It's like Legos. The whole system. Each module talks to the next, and if one goes down the others compensate."

Mason looked at the schematic, then at Delaney. "Nobody has ever put it that way before." He paused. "It's accurate, though."

The second week was the simulator. Jacobs ran it, and it turned out the quiet one was also the precise one: he froze the sim at the exact moment of each error and made them talk through what they would do before he let them try it. Engine-out at hover, engine-out at transition speed, clutch failure at cruise altitude. On the Osprey, a clutch failure was a catastrophic event. On the V-280,

Jacobs showed them the failed clutch disengaged cleanly, the remaining systems compensated, and the aircraft flew on. He ran the scenario six times.

On the sixth run, Garner landed it without a word from Jacobs and sat in the sim seat in the sudden quiet.

"That's why we switched," he said.

Jacobs closed his tablet. "That's why you switched."

The third week meant the first solo flights in the Valor. For Mark Delaney, the exercise included a low-level navigation exercise, skimming the deck of the Nevada desert. During the test flight, a sudden, unexpected dust storm boiled up, reducing visibility to near zero. In the Osprey, it would have meant a white-knuckle flight. The V-280's terrain-following radar guided Delaney through the brownout, allowing him to maintain a steady course on instruments alone. He landed back at Area 51 with deep respect for the new aircraft.

Next, it was Captain Garner's turn, minus the dust storm experience.

The last week of training was mission qualification. The two pilots practiced the specific clandestine profiles of Project Mogul, including long-range, low-altitude ingress, simulated insertions, and high-speed egress. They learned to trust the automation, not just the autopilot, but a system capable of executing complex flight profiles from takeoff to landing with minimal input. The final two days covered the aircraft's external lift capability: dual belly-mounted cargo hooks rated for six thousand pounds, deployable and releasable from the cockpit by either pilot or from the cabin station by a third crew member. Delaney ran the remote deployment sequence until it was automatic.

At last, with the pilots fully certified and qualified, the aircraft was ready for the flight to the base at S-3. When they arrived, the tow tug was waiting. The space once occupied by the V-22 was now the new home of its sleek successor, the V-280 Valor, Pandora 2.

As Garner and Delaney walked into the Ready Room, Director Renn was waiting.

"Just in time," she said, gesturing to a folder on her desk. "Prometheus hasn't been idle while you were in training. "

Chapter Nine

Stolen Thunder

Renn was already in her office at 0215 when the diplomatic channel opened.

She had been awake since midnight, not because anything was wrong but because the channel had been carrying low-level traffic for three days, the kind of traffic that was not a message but was not nothing either, and she had learned over years that the difference between background noise and a precursor signal was sometimes only visible in retrospect. She had decided not to find out in retrospect.

When the channel opened, she read what came through and sat still before making two calls. The first was to the diplomatic authorization system to arrange arrival credentials. The second was to the Ready Room duty channel.

***

She watched through the observation window: Garner arrived, reading the room from the doorway before he entered. Delaney was already at the terminal console.

Renn came down as a new arrival entered through the east corridor. She ushered him into the Ready Room.

Garner caught the distinctive features: platinum-blonde hair that might have been white in different light, unusually pale skin, and a face with the ageless quality that made estimating age impossible.

Garner looked at the strange arrival, and then at Renn with a question he did not ask aloud.

"Gentlemen," she said. "I need to introduce Xeriel. Together, we have a situation that requires urgent attention."

She pulled the satellite image onto the main screen. The map showed Eglin Air Force Base Auxiliary Field 3 identified as Duke Field.

"Two days ago," she said, "a small Nordic craft was on a monitoring mission over the Eglin reservation. Prometheus Applied Sciences had mapped that corridor from UAP tracking data obtained through their DOD contractor relationships. They positioned a modified contractor aircraft over the Eglin range and fired a directed-energy weapon at their target."

"The weapon," Renn explained, "was apparently derived from reverse-engineered alien technology."

She let that sit for a moment. Garner's expression did not change.

Delaney's hands rested on the keyboard as he contributed, "They've been getting help from the folks at the Puzzle Palace at Langley."

Garner nodded agreement.

"The spacecraft executed an automated emergency landing," Renn continued, "in an open area north of Duke Field on the Eglin reservation. Prometheus had a ground team pre-positioned with hunting permits as cover."

She glanced briefly at Xeriel. "Somehow they managed to access the spacecraft and overcome the pilot."

Renn continued, "The Air Force arrived before Prometheus could extract the craft from a military reservation where they had no authority."

"What about the ship?" Garner asked.

"The craft is intact, and it was transported by truck to a hangar on the main base," she said. "The pilot was moved to the base medical isolation facility, under sedation."

She turned to face both men fully. "The aliens have agreed not to start an interplanetary incident if we return what was stolen. Which means we have a very narrow window to retrieve their craft and its pilot from a secure military installation before they decide to come get it themselves."

Delaney's expression reflected the impossibility of the task.

Garner said: "What's the plan?"

Renn turned to the screen. "My sources indicate Eglin has scheduled a test flight for tonight. That's where we get involved." She turned to Garner. "Let's get Pandora 2 airborne as soon as possible. Mark, build us a cover of a standard training flight, with a stopover at Eglin."

"This is going to be interesting," Garner said as he was already moving toward the hangar for the preflight. Delaney resumed typing. He had some documents to create.

The new arrival was provided with standard military fatigues with a name tag reading "NILSEN" to imply an appropriate Scandinavian heritage.

***

An hour later, they met back in the Ready Room.

Delaney sat at the table and spread out the contents of a folder. "It's a really big base. All kinds of military aircraft from all over fly in and out all the time. But lately air traffic was restricted to daylight hours."

"Cover for the test flights, no doubt," Russ added.

"We've been cleared through the Pentagon to land at the base in conjunction with a training mission."

Captain Garner was considering the logistics. "The trip is twenty-four hundred miles. We'll need to refuel along the way. If the weather is good, cruising at 250 knots, we should make it in less than five hours."

"So, when do we leave?" Captain Garner asked.

Renn looked at her watch. "If you leave in the next two hours, we can get there before sundown."

"This should be most interesting," Captain Garner added as he finished his coffee.

The aircraft tug pulled Pandora 2 out into the sunlight, and the four passengers climbed aboard.

Mark checked the weather for the route and keyed in the flight plan, and in a few minutes received confirmation, and they went through the takeoff checklist.

Captain Garner hollered, "Clear!" and the twin turbojet engines roared to life. They climbed above the mountains and set a course for Valparaiso, Florida, by way of a refueling stop at Cannon Air Force Base near Clovis, New Mexico, at a cruising speed of 280 knots, with clearance for an altitude of eighteen-thousand feet for most of the flight.

A few hours later, Mark Delaney monitored the GPS navigation screen as they passed over Mobile, Alabama, and the Mississippi River. The clouds became thicker as they encountered the humid Gulf air.

A few minutes after they crossed into Florida, Captain Garner dialed in the Eglin Field approach frequency, and requested a landing sequence.

On landing, ground control directed them to a numbered space just off Taxiway A, in the area designated for securing transient and TDY aircraft, near the main airfield, southeast of Boatner Road.

Mark closed out the digital flight plan and shut down the navigation screen while Russ ran through the last of the landing checklist. Next, they chocked and tied down the aircraft.

The storage ramp was part of the controlled airfield zone, with restricted access and active patrols; an unavoidable hazard.

A car was parked nearby. A security guard rolled up in a golf cart and handed a key remote to Captain Garmen.

"Courtesy of the base director."

Garner and Renn proceeded to Base Operations, where Director Renn presented their Pentagon-issued Tier 1 security credentials to Base Operations.

Next, they drove to the transient quarters at the Tidewater Inn.

Once they found their room, Mark went to grab something to-go from the Burger King near the Base Exchange. Director Renn shared that their alien guest preferred vanilla ice cream.

It was still well before nightfall. Time for the rescue.

***

The E-Team's flight plan had been filed under a Pentagon logistics code reserved for inter-service systems evaluation, an authorization that generated no flags and created no curiosity. Garner had landed on the base's south side, and Pandora 2 was parked on the transient ramp under a cover story of routine V-280 training flights. The operations desk had logged their arrival. That part had been straightforward.

The documentation was more complicated.

Delaney had routed through four separate Pentagon proxy nodes to build the paper trail. He created a civilian contractor record for Xeriel under the name Axel Renner, a systems integration specialist attached to a real but obscure defense firm, Meridian Applied Dynamics, that held a legitimate Eglin access agreement. He backdated three contractor badge requests through the Eglin Visitor Control Center's scheduling queue, embedding them into a batch of actual requests submitted the prior week. The visitor log showed Renner had been credentialed for the base once before, sixty days prior, in a record Delaney had inserted cleanly enough that it would survive a spot audit.

He had also generated access orders for Hangar 910, a secondary maintenance facility adjacent to the King Hangar complex. The orders were keyed to the same Meridian contract number and signed with a digital signature belonging to a colonel at Wright-Patterson who Delaney on TDY in Europe. The orders authorized a small team to conduct an overnight inspection of Prometheus Applied Sciences' data relay equipment, which was a real installation Delaney located from cross-referencing base infrastructure records.

Xeriel's disguise was a practical compromise. Renn had made the call. The Nordic's height and coloring were impossible to fully conceal, but military bases were accustomed to tall contractors with pale complexions and a certain quiet intensity. Xeriel wore a fleece-lined field jacket over a dark pullover. His platinum hair was cropped tight under a ball cap. Mirrored aviator sunglasses handled the eyes. In daylight, he was conspicuous. In the base's fluorescent-lit interior corridors after 2100 hours, he was plausible.

Renn had studied the layout of the Eglin secure medical facility from satellite imagery and a floor plan Delaney had pulled from a construction archive. The facility was inside the 96th Medical Group complex on the north end of the base, but a designated wing had been walled off and assigned to the Air Force Research Laboratory under a classification header that did not appear on any public record. It was the kind of arrangement that existed in plain sight. The guards at the outer desk were regular security forces airmen. The inner corridor required a separate keycard.

Renn and Xeriel walked in together at 2118 hours.

She wore her field jacket open over a dark shirt, her security badge clipped at the collar and her Pentagon-issued supplemental identification tucked in her breast pocket alongside the fabricated Meridian orders. She carried a clipboard. It was the oldest prop in the world, and it worked because people on military installations did not question clipboards. They questioned uncertainty. Renn did not project uncertainty.

The airman at the outer desk was young, working a night shift, and had likely not had a visitor in hours. He looked up when they came in.

"Access review," Renn said, setting the clipboard on the counter and opening it to a page dense with checkboxes and printed names. "We need to verify the log for the subject in the restricted wing. Shouldn't take long."

The airman looked at the clipboard, then at her badge, then at Xeriel standing quietly at her shoulder. He picked up the phone.

Renn held still. She could feel Xeriel beside her, and she could feel something else: a low, directed pressure at the edge of her awareness, like a hand resting against a door. Xeriel was not forcing anything. He was simply present in the room in a way that went beyond physical space. Nordic telepathic projection was not hypnosis. It did not override cognition. What it did was quieter and more difficult to resist: it created the sensation that everything was already resolved, that the outcome was already known, and that the paperwork was merely a formality.

The airman set the phone down without dialing.

"Badge," he said.

Renn presented the supplemental ID. He scanned it. The badge reader chimed green, which was the correct result because Delaney had registered it correctly, but Renn was aware that the airman's attention had already begun to drift. He initialed the log, handed back the badge, and buzzed them through.

The inner corridor was painted institutional green and smelled of antiseptic and recycled air. Security cameras covered both ends. Renn kept her head down to avoid detection.

The restricted wing was behind a second key card reader. She used the card Delaney had cloned from a medical officer's badge. The card cleared.

The room at the end of the hall was guarded by a single airman in a folding chair who stood when he saw them coming. He was alert, even younger than the one at the outer desk, and his hand moved toward his radio before he caught himself. Whatever he was about to say, he did not say it.

Renn felt the pressure increase. Not from her. From Xeriel, beside her, steady and deliberate. This was not the soft ambient projection he had used at the outer desk. She could feel that too, a faint tension in the air near him, as though the effort required physical effort.

The airman looked at her badge for a long time. Then he nodded and stepped aside.

The pilot was on a medical bed, sedated, connected to a monitoring array that was clearly improvised. Someone had adapted standard vital-signs equipment to work on a patient whose physiology made the readouts meaningless. The screens showed numbers that meant nothing because they had been calibrated for humans.

Xeriel crossed to the bed. He placed his hand on the pilot's arm and said nothing aloud. Whatever passed between them took less than ten seconds.

The pilot's eyes opened.

Renn moved to the IV line and located the sedation feed. She pulled it. The pilot sat up slowly, aided by Xeriel, and Renn watched them communicate. The pilot understood the situation.

Getting out was harder than getting in. The pilot was unsteady from the sedation. Renn draped a medical gown over the pilot's frame. She kept her hand on the pilot's arm. To anyone watching, it looked like a supervised patient transfer.

The guard in the folding chair did not move as they passed. Renn did not look at him.

At the outer desk, the first airman was on his phone. He glanced up as they went by and looked back down at his phone without expression. The door opened. They walked out into the night air.

Renn exhaled once. She said nothing until they were fifty yards from the building.

"How long will they remember us?" she asked quietly.

Xeriel considered the question. "They will remember a review was conducted. The details will be difficult to reconstruct."

At midnight, all the lights on the field were turned off. They didn't want any witnesses.

The E-Team crew watched on an infrared camera as a few jeeps and Humvees moved around in front of the King Hangar, the largest hangar. Large hangar doors opened, and a dark object moved out onto the tarmac. The infrared camera confirmed it was the unmistakable form of a small alien spacecraft.

Garner handed Renn a scrambler-secured radio with an earpiece as she and the aliens stepped out of the plane and disappeared into the darkness.

Renn and her companions would need to cover a distance of half a mile, crossing over runway 12/30 past several security gates and a high fence topped with razor wire. They must be careful not to be caught on a security cameras or use a gate pass because it would leave a record for the investigation that was sure to follow.

Somehow, Renn and the alien pilots evaded all the hazards until at one point, Mark's camera picked up a guard patrolling behind a fence.

"Trouble!" Delaney warned as the infrared camera picked up a guard with a flashlight patrolling the fence outside the airfield.

Director Renn quietly replied, "Target in sight."

Mark watched as the pair hid in a shallow gully and waited as the guard passed by.

On directions from Director Renn, the tall aliens easily leaped over the last razor wire at the top of the eight-foot security fence and headed toward the hangar under cover of the night's darkness.

***

The Prometheus test flight was scheduled for 2230 hours, which Delaney confirmed by intercepting the operations request submitted to Eglin's base operations. The clearance had been granted under a Special Access Program identifier that Delaney could not fully decode, but the window was clear: a two-hour block, exclusive use of taxiway Echo-4 and the adjacent apron; no other aircraft movement was allowed. Prometheus had been flying the recovered Nordic craft. They had not been subtle about it because they believed they did not need to be.

The craft was rolled out of the King Hangar complex at 2205.

Delaney watched on his tablet from Pandora 2, pulling feeds from two base security cameras he had quietly tapped into. The alien craft was smaller than he had expected from the satellite imagery, roughly the dimensions of a large SUV, but flattened to a disc profile that made it seem wider than it was. It moved on a low-profile wheeled dolly towed by a military tractor. Two Prometheus technicians walked on either side. Four security force personnel flanked the convoy at the corners. The area around the King Hangar apron was lit with portable work lights on stands, and a Prometheus operations van was parked at the edge of the tarmac with a communications array on its roof.

"Eleven personnel total," Delaney said into his mic. "Four security, two tech, one ops van with probably two or three inside."

Renn had positioned herself with Xeriel and the pilot at the edge of Hangar 910's shadow line, forty meters from the King Hangar apron. The rescued pilot moved better now; the sedation had burned off, though Xeriel kept a steadying hand at the pilot's elbow. The pilot was in a Prometheus ground crew vest Delaney had sourced by locating a Prometheus contractor ID in a base administration database and matching it to a vest pulled from an unlocked equipment locker in Hangar 910. It was a loose fit. Nobody was going to look at it closely.

The access credential was a different problem. The tarmac around the craft had a formal security perimeter: a painted boundary line with posted signs, and the Prometheus security detail was enforcing it. To reach the craft, Xeriel and the pilot needed to cross that line with authorization, or cross it when the security detail's attention was elsewhere.

Renn had decided on both.

Delaney had pushed a set of Prometheus contractor badges into the system using a back-channel he had opened in the Meridian contract file. The badges were real in the sense that they would scan. They were not real in the sense that anyone at Prometheus had approved them. If a security guard ran a voice check to their operations van, the badges would not survive scrutiny.

Renn put her hand on the pilot's arm and squeezed once. The pilot looked at her. She nodded.

They walked out of the shadow line toward the tarmac perimeter. A security guard stepped to intercept them, hand raised.

"Systems check," Renn said. She held up the Prometheus badge without slowing. "Pre-flight sensor sweep. We're late."

The guard looked at the badge. He reached for his radio, then decided not to make the call.

Beside her, Renn felt the pressure she associated with Xeriel working: a calm, flat certainty that arrived in the guard's expression the same way it had at the medical facility, not confusion, not compliance, but a kind of authorized normalcy, as though the situation had already been resolved at a level above his responsibility. Xeriel did not project aggression. He projected administrative inevitability.

The guard scanned the badge. The reader chimed. He stepped back and waved them through.

They crossed the perimeter line at a walk. Renn kept her pace measured and her clipboard in front of her.

The craft sat on its dolly fifteen meters ahead, released from the tow tractor while the technicians ran their pre-flight checks. Up close, it was different from the satellite image. The surface was a dark, non-reflective material that absorbed the work lights rather than scattering them. There were no visible seams, no fasteners, no control surfaces. The technicians had attached a series of sensor leads to its underside with what appeared to be adhesive pads, and a cable run connected those leads to a laptop on a folding table nearby. The laptop was showing data that Renn glanced at without stopping. Prometheus had figured out propulsion telemetry.

The pilot moved to the craft's forward quadrant and pressed both palms flat against the surface. Nothing visible happened. Then a section of the hull shifted, the geometry changing with no mechanical indication, no sound, no gap, simply a reconfiguration of the surface into an opening. One of the Prometheus technicians looked up from the laptop and said something. Renn stepped between him and the craft.

"What are you doing? That's restricted access. Who authorized you?"

"Pentagon access review." Renn kept her voice flat. She put the clipboard on the technician's folding table without invitation and tapped the page. "Your flight window has been flagged for compliance review."

The technician stared at the clipboard. The page was dense with formatted text and a header that said AFRL INSPECTION PROTOCOL 7-C in bold. He had never seen that form before, which meant nothing, because he had not seen most of the forms that governed the program he was working on.

The distraction worked. Behind her, Xeriel and the rescued pilot were boarding the craft.

On the camera screen moments later, Mark and Russ watched as the ground crew scattered as the spaceship lifted off, just as it had for the previous tests.

This was different; it did not accelerate. It simply relocated. One moment it was on the dolly. The next, the dolly was empty and the sensor leads were dangling from nothing, and somewhere above the tarmac lights that Renn's eyes had not yet adjusted to see, the craft was gone.

In the resulting confusion, Renn was already moving. She walked at a deliberate pace back toward the perimeter line. The security personnel were converging on the dolly with and in the confusion of the lights and the shouting, none of them were looking at the woman in the field jacket walking away from the tarmac.

Renn crossed the tarmac line, walked through the hangar access road, and kept walking.

She keyed her radio. "I'm heading back."

Behind her, the Eglin flight line was waking up. She could hear it in the radio traffic bleeding through on the base frequency, the controlled urgency of people who had just lost a classified asset from a secured tarmac and were starting to account for personnel.

It would take them time to backtrack through the evening's events. By then, Pandora 2's flight plan would show a routine departure on a training block already filed, and the transient ramp records would be clean, and the badge logs would be the version Delaney left behind, which was close enough to the truth to survive an initial review and different enough from the truth in all the ways that mattered.

The next morning, the team calmly took the shuttle and joined other transient guests for breakfast at the Base Exchange. Calling the on-base taxi, they arrived at the parking ramp just as the field crew had finished refueling their plane. Mark climbed in and took his place in the Pandora 2 cockpit.

Checklist completed, Captain Garner called the tower for takeoff clearance while Mark checked the weather and keyed in the flight plan for New Mexico.

Flight plan approved and cleared for takeoff, the plane rose into the air. Minutes later, the altimeter read 9,000 feet and the heading was 290 degrees. They were heading for the fueling stop at Cannon, Air Force Base for refueling on the way home.

Chapter Ten

Gray Matter

The screen in the Ready Room displayed a surveillance still. A Gray, small and stooped, was being led in restraints between two armed escorts.

Director Kaela Renn clicked the remote, freezing the image. The timestamp read forty-eight hours earlier.

"Air Force intelligence unit," she said. "They're calling it 'a recovered biological asset.'"

Lieutenant Delaney leaned closer, eyes narrowing. The creature's oversized black eyes seemed to fix on the camera, even hooded.

Captain Russ Garner folded his arms. They were three days back from Eglin, and the ache of that mission was still in his shoulders. "We just got home."

"I know." Renn's voice did not soften. "Intercepts show an OSI convoy moving the asset tonight, toward a Prometheus handoff."

Delaney's jaw tightened. "Handoff for what?"

"Vivisection," Renn said. "Prometheus wants tissue samples and a working specimen, in that order of preference."

Garner straightened. "Where?"

"A private airstrip outside Dulce, New Mexico. The convoy routes overland, off the interstate, through the back country. Far enough from anything that nobody asks questions." Renn pulled up a terrain map. "Dulce has its own history. Local sightings going back decades. Nobody in that county blinks at strange lights anymore, which is exactly why Prometheus picked it."

"We're there before the convoy is," Renn said. "Wheels up within the hour."

Delaney was already pulling up convoy logistics on his tablet. "OSI escort, probably four to six personnel, standard rolling-frequency comms. I can work with that. What's our window?"

"The convoy stops to rest at a private ranch staging point eleven miles short of the airstrip," Renn said. "That's our intercept point. After that, they're inside Prometheus security and we lose our chance."

"Extraction after we get the Gray?" Garner asked.

"Mother ship holds position over the Jicarilla highlands, north of the ranch. We deliver, they receive, we're gone before Prometheus knows the convoy never arrived." Renn closed the file.

***

Pandora 2 set down at a disused agricultural strip nine miles from the staging ranch, the V-280's rotors kicking dust across sage and scrub as Garner brought her in low and quiet. The flight had been short enough that nobody had time to get tired, which Garner counted as a mercy after the marathon to Eglin.

Delaney had the laptop open before the rotors finished spinning down. "Ranch security uses a private network, not military grade. Give me ten minutes."

He got in faster than that. By the time Renn had changed into a contractor's coverall with a forged livestock inspection credential, Delaney had pulled the convoy's arrival window, the staging building layout, and a personnel roster.

"Four OSI," he said. "Sergeant in charge is a man named Morrison. Six years in, spotless file until two months ago. Then there's a flag. Financial counseling referral."

Renn looked up. "Compromised?"

"Looks like it. Daughter started college last fall. Tuition's not cheap." Delaney scrolled. "Somebody's been paying him to look the other way at convenient moments. My money's on Prometheus."

"Then he already knows what he's carrying," Renn said quietly. "That makes this easier or harder. We'll find out which."

***

The staging building was a converted equipment barn, lit by sodium lamps and parked vehicles. Renn crossed the gravel yard at an even pace, clipboard in hand, while Delaney monitored from a ridge a quarter mile out with a directional antenna and a spoofing rig.

A guard intercepted her at the door. "Help you, ma'am?"

"Livestock and wildlife compliance," Renn said, holding up the credential. "Got a report of contaminated cargo crossing federal land near here. Routine check, shouldn't take long."

The guard's eyes flicked toward the barn, then back to her. He didn't move.

A second man stepped out from behind the transport truck. Square shoulders, sergeant's bearing, tired around the eyes in a way that had nothing to do with the hour. Mid-forties, grey at the temples, built like a man who'd kept up the PT long after the Air Force stopped requiring it.

His name was Sergeant Daniel Morrison.

"This is a federal convoy," Morrison said. "Wrong agency, wrong night."

"Then you won't mind me confirming that with your duty officer," Renn said, unbothered. "Or we can do this the slow way, where I call in a hazmat hold and your whole convoy sits here till morning."

Morrison studied her. Something in his posture said he had run this calculation before, with other people, for other reasons. "Sergeant Morrison. Step inside. Five minutes."

Delaney's voice came through her earpiece, low. "He bought it for now. Watch him. Tablet shows he just queried his own chain of command, not yours. He's checking something else."

Inside, the Gray sat on a low transport pallet, restrained at wrists and ankles, the hood removed for transport but the lighting kept dim. It did not move when Renn entered. Its eyes tracked her without turning its head.

"You're not wildlife compliance," Morrison said once the door was shut.

"No," Renn agreed.

Morrison's hand drifted to his sidearm, then stopped. He looked at the Gray, then back at her, and something in his face changed, the particular exhaustion of a man who had been waiting for this conversation without knowing it.

"I know what Prometheus wants it for," he said. "I've known for two weeks."

"Then you also know what happens to you once they have it," Renn said. "They don't keep loose ends around. A sergeant who delivered the asset and saw too much is a liability, not an asset."

Morrison's jaw worked. "My daughter's tuition is paid through next spring because of them."

"And paid through nothing after that," Renn said. "You're not buying her an education. You're renting silence, and the rent's about to come due in a way you won't like."

He didn't answer. His eyes went to the Gray again.

Renn lowered her voice. "I'm not here to arrest you, Sergeant. I'm here to take that asset somewhere Prometheus never finds it, and to give you a story that gets you and your team home clean. After that, what you do with what you know is your business."

Morrison's radio crackled. He didn't answer it.

"Ten minutes," he said finally. "Then I'm calling it in as scheduled, whether you're done or not."

He stepped outside to hold the door.

***

The restraints were a problem Delaney had not fully solved from the ridge. Up close, the locks were a sealed military pattern with rolling tamper codes, nothing like the simpler hardware from Eglin.

"Working it," Delaney said in her ear, voice tight with concentration. "Tamper detection resets every failed attempt. I need clean tries, not guesses."

The first tumbler gave. The second reset the whole sequence.

"Damn it." Sweat had started at his hairline a quarter mile away, and Renn could hear it in his breathing. "Sixty more seconds."

Renn knelt beside the Gray instead of waiting on the lock. She had not touched it yet, not directly, and she understood why Xeriel's people called this kind of contact something gentler than what waited for her now.

"Can you help me," she said, "with the restraint?"

The Gray's head turned, slow and deliberate, and its eyes met hers, and the moment her hand closed over its thin fingers the world tilted sideways. *No clean signal, no shaped thought, just a flood: years compressed into seconds, fluorescent rooms, needles, the particular cruelty of curiosity without consent, and underneath all of it something that was not quite fear and not quite resignation but close to both.* Renn's vision blurred. She held on anyway.

The restraint hummed at a frequency she felt in her molars and released.

She pulled back, breathing hard, one hand pressed briefly to her temple.

"You good?" Delaney's voice, sharper now.

"Fine," she said, which was not entirely true. "Moving."

***

Morrison was still in the doorway when they came out, the Gray walking unsteadily between Renn and the wall, favoring one side.

"Five minutes early," Morrison said.

"Lucky for both of us," Renn answered.

His radio crackled again, a duty check this time, routine. He keyed it without looking away from her. "Convoy secure, resuming staging on schedule." A pause, then he added, off the radio, just for her: "There's a maintenance gate on the north fence. Unlocked since I had a man through it an hour ago. Nobody's watching it."

"Why," Renn asked, "are you helping us?"

"Because you're right about the rent," Morrison said. "And because I'd rather sleep knowing I did one thing that wasn't for them." He looked at the Gray one more time. "Go."

***

The maintenance gate put them a quarter mile from the ridge where Delaney waited with the antenna packed and the rendezvous coordinates already loaded. Garner had Pandora 2 spun up and waiting at the agricultural strip, running lights dark.

"Contact bearing three-one-zero, low," Delaney reported once they were airborne, watching the sensor return resolve into a shape against the night sky. "Range four miles and closing."

The mother ship met them over the Jicarilla highlands the way it had over the Gulf months earlier, a long shadow against the stars, descending without sound, matching their airspeed with a precision Garner had still not gotten used to.

"Hoist's out," Delaney said, working the basket controls from the cabin while Garner held position. The Gray went into the basket without resistance, the injured wrist tucked against its body, and the line ran out across the gap between aircraft and ship.

A portal opened, seamless, and received the basket. The line went taut, held a moment, then the tension dropped out of the cable.

The portal closed. The ship rose, unhurried, and the cloud cover took it.

Garner brought Pandora 2 around onto a heading for home. Nobody spoke for a while.

"Morrison's going to file something," Delaney said eventually. "Question is what."

"Whatever keeps his team clean and his conscience quiet," Renn said. "He's not going to volunteer the rest. Men like that carry it instead." She rubbed her temple, still feeling the echo of the contact behind her eyes. "He'll need watching. Prometheus isn't going to write off a missed handoff without asking questions, and a sergeant with a daughter in college is exactly the kind of loose end they clean up."

Garner glanced back from the cockpit. "That a problem for tonight, or a problem for later?"

"Later," Renn said. "Tonight we got it right."

She settled back against the bulkhead, hands steady now, and watched the New Mexico desert give way to the dark line of mountains that meant home.

Chapter Eleven

Chain of Custody

Three days after the convoy, Sergeant Morrison sat in a windowless room at Cannon Air Force Base, sweating through his dress uniform. The wool collar felt tighter than regulation, as if the room had lost a few percent of oxygen. He resisted the urge to roll his shoulders; slight movements would be noted in rooms like this.

Across the table were two men. The first wore an Air Force colonel's insignia. The second wore an expensive suit and the kind of smile that never reached his eyes.

"Let's go through it again," the colonel said. His nameplate read HARTWELL. "You diverted the convoy off its route at the ranch staging point. Why?"

Morrison kept his voice steady. "Federal compliance flagged a contamination concern on the cargo manifest. Standard protocol is to isolate and verify."

"Federal compliance." The suited man leaned forward. "Would that be the woman who showed you the inspection credential? Or the contractor with her?"

Morrison felt the heat gather between his shoulder blades, the way it did right before a live-fire evaluation, when you knew a mistake was coming and there was no pause button.

"Yes, sir," he answered.

"Describe them."

"White female, forties, tall, white or platinum blonde hair. Professional demeanor. The contractor was male, younger, carried a laptop and an antenna rig he said was for signal verification."

"Names?"

"I don't recall. She showed credentials: a federal livestock and wildlife compliance badge, properly formatted, current. She knew the convoy's staging location and the route we were running, information that's classified and compartmented. I verified what I could verify, sir."

The suited man's smile widened. "That's unfortunate, Sergeant, because the regional wildlife compliance office has no record of issuing any such inspection. The credentials were fake. Very good fakes, good enough to fool our verification protocols. The contamination flag was fake. And whoever briefed them had access to information they shouldn't have had."

Morrison's hands tightened on the armrest. "Sir, I followed protocol. The orders appeared legitimate."

"Appeared." Colonel Hartwell tapped a folder. "Sergeant, you've been with OSI for six years. You've transported classified materials forty-three times. Never once have you deviated from authorized routes. Until the ranch."

The suited man laid a photograph on the table. One of Morrison's team members had taken it on his phone before going outside. Grainy, taken at an angle, but clear enough.

Morrison stood aside while two figures led the Gray toward an exit.

"That's you," the man said. "Watching them take it. Not stopping them. Not calling for backup. Just ... watching."

Morrison fixed his eyes on the edge of the table. He'd learned early that staring at evidence never helped; details lodged themselves where they didn't belong and came back later, uninvited.

"I was told ..."

"You were told a story," Colonel Hartwell interrupted. "And you believed it. Or you wanted to believe it. The question is why."

Silence.

The suited man folded his hands. "I'm Marcus Webb. Prometheus Applied Sciences. We had a contract to receive that package for analysis. DoD approved, fully authorized. Because of your ... lapse in judgment ... that contract is now void, and we're out seven million dollars in R&D costs."

The name landed like a dropped tool, dull and final. Morrison kept his posture locked. The same Prometheus had wired him fifteen thousand dollars to report convoy schedules.

Webb observed him. "You seem nervous, Sergeant."

"I'm being accused of losing a classified asset, sir."

"It is," Webb agreed. "Unless there's an explanation. Something that makes sense of your choices." He paused. "Were you coerced? Threatened? Did they have something on you?"

There it was. The lifeline: the out. His hands stayed flat on the armrests, fingers spread just enough to stop them from curling. He'd seen men take that lifeline before, and they always took it too quickly.

Morrison could say yes. He could say the woman threatened him and forced him to comply. It would explain everything; shift the blame. But it would also trigger an investigation. They'd dig into his background, his finances, his phone records. And they'd find the Prometheus payment.

If he took the lifeline, he'd drown anyway.

"No, sir," Morrison said quietly. "I made a judgment call based on the information presented. I guess I was wrong."

Webb studied him for a long moment. Then he stood. "Colonel, I think we're done here. The Sergeant made an error. A costly one. But unless there's evidence of deliberate sabotage ..."

"There isn't," Hartwell said. "Just incompetence."

Webb nodded. "Then I'll let the Air Force handle its personnel matters. We'll file our loss claim with DoD and move on." He looked at Morrison one last time. "Sergeant, I hope your next assignment goes better. For everyone's sake."

They left. Morrison stayed seated until the hum of the ventilation system became the loudest thing in the room. Only then did he realize he'd been holding his core tight, braced as if for an impact that never came.

He'd survived. Barely. But Prometheus knew. Webb knew. That last look had said it all: We own you. Don't forget it.

***

Four hours later, Morrison sat in his truck in the Cannon parking lot, staring at a message on his phone. He rested his forearms on the steering wheel and forced his breathing into the same count he used on the range. In through the nose. Hold. Out slow. It worked, mostly.

The text had arrived ten minutes earlier. Unknown number.

You made the right choice in that room. Keep making it. The woman from the ranch.

Kaela Renn had used top secret resources to get his number and to disguise the source.

His phone buzzed. A second message.

Webb will contact you within forty-eight hours. He'll ask you to do something. Refuse. We'll handle the rest.

Morrison typed: Who are you?

The response came instantly.

Someone who knows what you took from Prometheus. And someone who can make sure they never find out. Stay clean, Sergeant. We'll be in touch.

Morrison deleted the messages, but his hands were still shaking.

He was now caught between two forces: Prometheus, who thought they owned him, and whoever R represented, who actually did.

Meanwhile, Director Kaela Renn set her phone down and looked across the conference table to Delaney.

"He held," Delaney said, monitoring the Cannon security feed on his laptop. "Webb tried to give him an out. Morrison didn't take it."

"Good." Renn pulled up a file on her tablet. "What do we have on Webb?"

"Marcus Webb, VP of Special Projects at Prometheus. Former DIA, forced retirement after a security incident in 2018. Now he runs Prometheus's black acquisitions unit. Handles the contracts."

"And the seven million dollar claim?"

"Real," Delaney said. "Prometheus had a contract to analyze the Gray entity, DoD authorized, signed by General Briggs. We just stole seven million dollars' worth of their work."

Renn nodded slowly. "They'll come after it. After us."

"They already are." Delaney pulled up another file. "Prometheus filed a formal complaint with DoD yesterday. They're claiming the package was intercepted by a rival contractor using forged credentials. They want an investigation."

"Let them investigate," Renn said. "Morrison's story holds. No names, no physical evidence, no trail back to us. The ranch's perimeter footage was corrupted, remember?"

Delaney smirked. "Terrible maintenance out there."

"And Morrison?"

"Trapped," Delaney said. "If he flips on us, we burn him with the Prometheus payments. If he flips on Prometheus, they burn him with the convoy intel he leaked. He's locked in place."

"Which means he's vulnerable." Renn stood, pacing. "Webb's going to push him. Try to turn him into an active asset instead of a passive one. When that happens, Morrison's going to break or push back. Either way, he becomes a problem."

"So what do we do?"

Renn was quiet for a moment, thinking. "We give him a way out. A real one."

"How?"

Delaney leaned forward. "Make him the victim instead of the perpetrator. If we can prove Prometheus targeted him deliberately, that they researched his vulnerabilities, his daughter's college timeline, his financial pressure points, then Morrison wasn't a willing conspirator. He was groomed."

Renn nodded slowly. "Proof," she said.

"Prometheus needs Morrison to stay quiet about his mistakes. We need Morrison to stay quiet about us. But Morrison needs protection from both of us." She let that sink in. "What if we gave him something more valuable than silence?"

Delaney frowned. "Like what?"

"Proof that Prometheus set him up. That they paid him to report convoy details specifically so they could intercept packages later. That he was a patsy, not a co-conspirator."

"You want to flip the script. Make Morrison the victim."

"Exactly. We feed him evidence that Prometheus planned to frame him from the start. He takes it to OSI Internal Affairs, cooperates fully, and walks away with immunity in exchange for testimony."

Delaney's eyes widened. "That burns Prometheus's entire operation. Webb, Briggs, all of it."

"Yes," Renn said. "And it removes Morrison as a threat. He's no longer trapped between us. He's a protected witness."

"But Morrison has to agree to it. He has to be willing to testify."

"He will be," Renn said quietly. "Once Webb makes his move. Morrison will realize he's never getting out from under Prometheus unless someone helps him. That's when we make contact."

Delaney nodded slowly. "This is risky. If Morrison talks before we're ready ..."

"He won't. He's too smart for that." Renn pulled up a message on her phone, began typing. "But we need to monitor Webb's next steps. Can you tap Prometheus's internal comms?"

"Already on it," Delaney said. "I've got a backdoor into their contractor management system. If Webb reaches out to Morrison, I'll know."

"Good. Let me know the second he does."

***

Two days later, Morrison's phone rang: Unknown number.

He answered. "Morrison."

"Sergeant, this is Marcus Webb. We met at Cannon."

Morrison's grip tightened on the phone as he recognized the voice. "Mr. Webb."

"I wanted to follow up on our conversation. See how you're holding up."

"I'm fine, sir."

"Good. Good." Webb's voice was smooth, practiced. "Listen, I know that was a tough interview. A lot of pressure. But I want you to know, Prometheus doesn't hold you responsible for what happened."

Morrison said nothing.

"In fact," Webb continued, "we see you as a valuable asset. Someone who understands the ... complexities of this work. And we'd like to continue our relationship."

There it was.

"What kind of relationship?" Morrison asked carefully.

"The same as before. Situational awareness. You let us know when certain packages are being moved, and we compensate you for your time. Simple. Discreet. Enough to cover, say, a semester of tuition. Your daughter starts college in the fall, doesn't she?"

"That's espionage, Mr. Webb."

Webb laughed. "It's consulting, Sergeant. DoD contractors consult with military personnel all the time. It's how the system works."

"I can't do that."

Silence on the other end. When Webb spoke again, his voice had lost its warmth.

"Sergeant, I'm trying to be helpful here. The Air Force is reviewing your file. Questions are being asked about your judgment, your reliability. A positive reference from Prometheus could go a long way toward smoothing things over. But if we have to tell DoD that you were uncooperative, that you obstructed our contract ..."

"Are you threatening me?"

"I'm clarifying your options. You help us, we help you. You refuse, and we have documentation of our previous arrangement: emails, payment records, meeting logs. The way those documents read, Sergeant, they make you look like an active participant in industrial espionage, not someone who made an error in judgment. Your choice is how the Air Force interprets them."

Morrison felt his chest tighten. This was it: the moment Renn had predicted.

"I need time to think," he said.

"You have twenty-four hours."

The call ended.

Morrison sat in his truck, staring at the phone. Then he opened his messages and typed:

He called. Wants me to keep reporting. 24 hours to decide.

The response from R came in seconds.

Don't decide yet. Meet me tonight. 2200 hours. Parking lot C, northwest corner. Come alone.

Morrison hesitated. Then he typed back:

How do I know this isn't a trap?

You don't. But it's the only way out you have. See you at 2200.

***

At 2200 hours the parking lot was empty except for two vehicles: Morrison's truck and a dark sedan with tinted windows. The scene was silent except for the distant chirping of crickets and the hum of the sodium light fixtures.

Morrison killed the engine and waited.

The sedan's door opened. The woman from the ranch stepped out. Same platinum hair, same unhurried pace. She walked to his passenger door and slid into the seat.

"Sergeant Morrison," she said. "Thank you for coming."

"Who are you?"

"That doesn't matter," Renn replied. "I'm part of an oversight unit. We handle situations that fall outside normal chains of command."

Morrison was not impressed. "Like stealing classified prisoners from OSI convoys?"

"Like preventing classified prisoners from being weaponized by defense contractors." Renn pulled out a tablet, showing it to him. "This is what Prometheus was going to do with that Gray."

Morrison looked at the screen. Files. Test protocols.

"They were going to vivisect it," Renn said quietly. "Take it apart piece by piece to understand how its neural system processes information. Then they would use that research to build weapons that target human nervous systems."

Morrison's expression revealed hints of revulsion.

"Webb didn't tell you that," Renn continued. "He told you it was R&D. Analysis. He made it sound clean. But Prometheus doesn't do clean work, Sergeant. They do profitable work."

Morrison handed the tablet back. "Why are you showing me this?"

"Because Webb just tried to reactivate you. And you need to understand what you're choosing between." Renn pulled up another file. "These are the payment records linking you to Prometheus. Fifteen thousand dollars, plus two smaller payments before that. Total of twenty-two thousand over the past six weeks."

Morrison's throat was dry. "You're going to turn me in."

"No," Renn said. "I'm going to give you a choice. You can work for Webb, keep taking his money, and eventually get caught when OSI Internal Affairs figures out what you've been doing. Or you can do something else."

"Like what?"

"Testify. Go to OSI Internal Affairs, tell them everything: how Prometheus approached you, offered money, pressured you into compliance. That you were compromised but not complicit. Then you cooperate fully, provide evidence, and in exchange, you get immunity and witness protection."

Morrison stared at her. "They'll never believe I'm innocent."

"They will if my organization gives them proof that Prometheus set you up from the start." Renn reached into a pocket and held up a flash drive. "These are internal Prometheus communications showing they targeted you specifically. They researched your financials, found out you had a daughter starting college, knew you'd be vulnerable to cash offers. They cultivated you, Sergeant. You were the mark, not the co-conspirator."

Morrison took the drive, his hands still trembling. "Why would you do this for me?"

"Because you made a choice at the ranch," Renn said. "Webb offered you a lifeline in that interview room. You didn't take it. You could've blamed us, tried to save yourself, triggered an investigation that would've exposed both of us. But you didn't. You took the hit." She paused. "That earned my respect. But I'd be lying if I said helping you wasn't also strategic. Burning Prometheus protects our operation. Your testimony makes that possible. So yes, Sergeant. I'm helping you because you deserve it, and because I need you. Both things are true."

"I didn't have a choice."

"Everyone has a choice. You made yours. And that's the difference between us and Prometheus: we asked. They take." Renn opened the door. "You've got twelve hours before Webb wants an answer. Think about what kind of man you want to be when this is over. If you decide to testify, call this number." She handed him a card with only a number. "If you decide to work for Webb, throw the drive away and forget we talked."

She stepped out of the truck.

"Director," Morrison said. "The Gray. Where is it now?"

Renn stopped at the door, then looked back at him. "Does it matter to you?"

"I watched them load it into that warehouse. I keep thinking about what Webb was going to do to it." Morrison's voice was quiet. "I need to know it's not suffering because of my mistakes."

"It's safe," Renn said. "We returned it to its people. It's home now, Sergeant. Where it belongs."

"And your operation? You're any different from Prometheus?"

"I'd like to think so. But that's a question you'll have to answer for yourself." She opened the sedan door. "The difference is, we're giving you a choice. Webb never did."

She drove away.

Morrison sat alone, holding the flash drive and the card, weighing two futures. One where he kept lying, kept hiding, kept working for people who saw him as a tool. One where he told the truth and tried to claw his way back to something clean.

At 0800 the next morning, with two hours remaining on Webb's ultimatum, Sergeant Morrison walked into the OSI Internal Affairs office and asked to speak to an investigator.

***

His daughter would start college in three months. He wanted to be someone she could be proud of when she graduated.

Morrison set the flash drive on the investigator's desk.

"My name is Sergeant Daniel Morrison," he said. "And I need to report a security breach. Mine."

He had a story to tell.

***

Director Renn sat in her office at S-3, reading the classified brief that had just been delivered.

SUBJECT: OSI Investigation, Prometheus Applied Sciences

STATUS: Active. Six arrests pending. Contracts suspended.

WITNESS: Sgt. Morrison (protective custody, full cooperation)

RECOMMENDATION: Expand to Major General Jonathan Briggs, USA, USASOC, Fort Liberty (oversight failure, contract irregularities)

She set the brief down and looked at Mark Delaney, who sat across from her.

"Morrison came through," Delaney said. "He gave them everything. Webb, Briggs, the payments, the convoy intel. Prometheus's entire black acquisitions unit is getting rolled up."

"And Morrison?"

"Immunity deal, early retirement with full benefits, relocation assistance. He's out. Clean."

Renn nodded slowly. "Good."

"General Briggs is going to know this came from us," Delaney said. "The timing, the evidence, the way it all came together. He'll know we orchestrated it."

"Yes, he will." Renn's expression was grim. "Briggs can't touch us without exposing himself. But he can make our lives difficult. Funding requests delayed. Security clearances re-investigated. Operational approvals suddenly requiring three more signatures. He'll wage a bureaucratic war, and we can't fight back without revealing why we burned Prometheus."

"So we won, but we're paying for it."

"We always pay for it," Renn said quietly. "The question is whether the cost is worth it. In this case? Yes. Morrison gets his life back, Prometheus loses their black acquisitions capability, and one Gray entity isn't being vivisected in a lab. That's worth some paperwork headaches."

Delaney smiled. "You really did give Morrison a way out."

"I gave him a choice," Renn corrected. "He's the one who took it." She stood, walked to the window overlooking the hangar. "Besides, burning Prometheus was always the plan. Morrison just gave us a cleaner way to do it."

"You think he'll be okay? Morrison?"

"I think he'll sleep better than he has in months." Renn turned back to Delaney. "And we'll sleep better knowing Prometheus can't intercept another convoy."

Her phone buzzed. A message from an unknown number.

Thank you. M

Renn typed back:

Stay safe, Sergeant.

She deleted the thread and pocketed the phone. Then she walked to the hangar.

The maintenance crew was already working. Director Renn stood back and watched them remove the tail number. The aircraft that had carried the alien to freedom was being erased, repainted, reborn with a new identity.

It was in the nature of their work. They couldn't operate in the light. They moved, adapted, and vanished when necessary. Every victory came with a price: sometimes measured in bureaucratic warfare with generals like Briggs, sometimes measured in the identities burned to stay invisible.

As the old registration dissolved, a fresh one took its place.

Garner approached, holding updated paperwork. "New tail number, new transponder code, new paper trail registered. By tomorrow morning, the previous aircraft never existed."

"Good," Renn said, watching the painter's work, replacing the N number. "We can't keep doing this forever. Eventually, we'll run out of shadows to hide in."

"Maybe," Garner said. "But not today."

It was one more ghost in a long line of ghosts, one more secret added to the pile he never talked about.

But Morrison was free. The Gray alien was home. And Prometheus would think twice before intercepting another convoy.

For now, that was enough.

Chapter Twelve

Sonora Intercept

Lieutenant Mark Delaney was running fuel supply calculations at his desk in the Ready Room. Director Renn walked in carrying a tablet and an urgent expression.

"We have a situation," she said without preamble. "Gray reconnaissance craft went down in the Sonoran Desert, forty miles south of the border. Mexican military is en route, but a Prometheus recovery team is closer."

Captain Russ Garner looked up from the maintenance log he had been reviewing. "How much closer?"

"Prometheus has a thirty-minute lead. Maybe less." Renn pulled up a map on the wall screen. "The crash site is here, just outside Caborca. Remote area, but not remote enough."

Delaney studied the coordinates. "That's six hundred fifty miles from here. Even with auxiliary tanks, we're pushing maximum range. Prometheus has a forward operating base disguised as a mining survey camp about sixty miles north. They're already rolling. We'll need to secure that craft before either party arrives."

"Exactly why we're leaving now," Renn said. "Captain, how fast can you get us in the air?"

Garner was already moving toward the door. "Fifteen minutes after the aux tanks are mounted."

"They are," Renn confirmed. "I already alerted the ground crew."

Delaney grabbed his flight bag and tablet. "What about clearance? We can't file a flight plan for an incursion into Mexican territory."

"We're not filing anything," Renn replied. "This is a ghost flight all the way. In and out before anyone realizes we were there."

***

Twenty minutes later, Pandora 2 was airborne and climbing through ten thousand feet on a heading of one-six-zero degrees. Delaney had calculated their fuel burn rate three times, and each time the numbers came back uncomfortably tight.

"We'll reach the target in about four and a half hours," he reported. "That gives us maybe forty minutes on station before we have to turn back, or we'll be running on fumes."

"Then we don't loiter," Garner said. "We get in, hook the craft, and get out."

Renn sat in one of the rear crew seats, her eyes closed in what might have been meditation or concentration. Delaney had learned not to interrupt her during these moments. He suspected she was doing more than just thinking.

They crossed into Mexican airspace at fifteen thousand feet, well above the coverage of most ground-based radar. The VEIL Gen 2 system was active, creating ghost returns that suggested they were sixty miles east of their actual position.

"Terrain ahead," Garner announced as the desert mountains appeared on the horizon. "Dropping to five hundred feet for the approach."

The aircraft descended smoothly, and Delaney felt his stomach rise as they leveled off just above the desert floor. At this altitude, they were below most radar coverage, but also dangerously close to the unforgiving terrain.

"GAD is active," Delaney said, monitoring the Gravimetric Anomaly Detector. "Scanning for the craft's signature."

"How did Prometheus pick this up so fast?" Delaney asked. "They'd need their own gravimetric sensors."

"They do," Renn said. "Reverse-engineered from recovered technology. They've got a network of monitoring stations along the border specifically to detect anomalies like this. It's how they stay ahead of official recovery teams."

The detector remained quiet for several minutes as they raced south. Then a spike appeared on his screen.

"Contact. Bearing one-seven-two, range eighteen miles. Gravitational distortion consistent with Gray propulsion technology."

"That's our target," Renn said from behind them, her eyes closed. "We need to move fast." Renn opened her eyes. A muscle in her jaw was tight. "The pilot is alive but injured.

Garner didn't ask how she knew. "Fifteen minutes to target."

Delaney switched his attention to other sensors. "MSSA shows three vehicles approaching from the north. Range twenty-two miles. They're moving fast on the highway."

"Prometheus," Renn said. "They'll be there in twenty minutes."

"And the Mexican military?" Garner asked.

Delaney checked the tactical display. "Two helicopters, looks like UH-60 variants, bearing two-two-zero, range forty miles. Flying slow and wide. Looks like they're still coordinating with ground units."

"Because they don't know what they're looking for yet," Renn said. "Prometheus has real-time tracking from their network of sensors. They knew the craft was in distress before it even hit the ground. The Mexican military is responding to a civilian report of something falling from the sky. They're flying reconnaissance protocols, not a hot extraction."

A classic Tic Tac shape about forty feet long came into view as they crested a low ridge. It sat in a shallow arroyo, its normally smooth surface scorched and damaged, one end partially buried in sand.

Garner brought them to a hover two hundred yards from the wreck. "MSSA shows a single heat signature inside the craft. Looks human-sized but the thermal pattern is off."

"That's our pilot," Renn confirmed. She was already unstrapping. "Lieutenant, keep scanning for those vehicles. Captain, I need you to position for cargo hook extraction once we assess the damage."

Renn opened the crew door and dropped onto the sand. Delaney watched through the external cameras as she approached the downed craft with careful steps. She placed her hand on the hull near what might have been an access panel, and after a moment, a section of the craft's surface seemed to dissolve.

A Gray alien form emerged slowly, moving with obvious difficulty. Even from the camera's distance, Delaney could see one of the alien's arms hung at an odd angle. The being's large eyes fixed on Renn, and for a long moment neither moved. Then the Gray nodded once.

Renn helped the pilot move away from the craft and toward Pandora 2.

"Vehicles just came into view," Garner reported. "Three Suburbans, moving fast. Five minutes out."

The Gray climbed aboard with Renn's assistance and moved to one of the rear crew seats. Delaney tried not to stare as the being worked the restraint buckles with three-fingered hands, moving with surprising efficiency despite its injuries.

Then the alien's head dropped.

The large eyes lost focus, going distant in a way that had nothing to do with the landscape outside. Renn was beside it immediately, one hand on its forearm, and whatever she made contact with was not the near-conversation she had described in the briefing room back at S-3. This was something else. Delaney could see the effort in her posture, the way her free hand went flat against her own thigh like she was bracing against pressure.

The Gray's consciousness was retreating. That was the only word Delaney could find for what he was watching. And Renn was following it inward, pushing the headache that had started the moment she touched the hull outside, pushing past it to hold the channel open.

The mother ship needed to locate them. Without a signal from the pilot, it would not know where to look.

Garner glanced back once and said nothing. He had noticed what Delaney noticed: Renn's hand had gone white at the knuckles.

"Cargo hooks," she said. "We lift it now."

Delaney already had the deployment panel open.

Garner maneuvered Pandora 2 directly over the wreckage. Delaney remotely deployed the dual cargo hooks, guiding them down toward the hard points on the craft's hull that Renn had somehow identified during her approach.

"Hooks attached," Delaney reported. "But Director, this thing has to weigh tons. That's beyond our rated capacity, not to mention the fuel requirement."

"The craft's anti-gravity system compensates for its mass through the same field technology that allows it to fly," Renn said. "Once we're airborne, it'll feel lighter than it is. Trust me."

Garner gradually increased power to the engines. "Taking up the strain now."

The engines whined as they pulled against the weight. For a moment, nothing happened. Then the craft broke free from the sand.

It did not feel light.

"Director." Garner's voice was quiet and specific. "Your anti-gravity field isn't holding. I've got real mass on the hooks."

Renn's jaw tightened. She looked at the alien beside her, then back at the instrument panel ahead. "The system took damage in the crash. It's compensating partially. How bad?"

"I can carry it. I don't know for how long, or what it does to our fuel burn." Garner watched the engine readouts climb. The torque was building across both shafts at a rate that didn't match what three thousand pounds should demand. "This feels like eight, nine thousand pounds. Maybe more."

"Get us north," Renn said. "We don't have time to set it down."

Garner accelerated north, climbing to five hundred feet with the craft suspended beneath them.

"MSSA: Suburbans are at the site," Delaney announced. "Personnel dismounting."

Through the camera feed, they could see armed men in tactical gear spreading out around the now-empty arroyo, looking up at Pandora 2 with weapons raised but not firing.

"They won't shoot," Renn said. "They know what they're looking at, and they know shooting at us risks bringing down what they want to recover."

Delaney was already working a different problem.

The MSSA wasn't just painting bodies and weapons. The lead Suburban was broadcasting: a tight-band position feed pushing their current coordinates to a remote receiver somewhere northwest. He tracked the signal for ten seconds to confirm it wasn't random traffic. It wasn't. Someone on the other end was listening, and if that receiver had air assets attached, Pandora 2's route home was already on a map.

"They've got a tracker on the lead vehicle," he said. "Active feed. Someone's receiving their position in real time."

Renn didn't look away from the Gray. "Spoof it."

Easy to say. Delaney pulled the signal's frequency off the MSSA and pushed it into the electronic warfare panel, one hand managing the cargo weight readouts while the other built the spoof. He had to match the transmission cadence exactly or the receiver would see the gap and know something had changed. He got close. Close enough.

"Spoof is running," he said. "As far as their receiver knows, that Suburban is parked outside Hermosillo and has been for the last six minutes."

"How long will it hold?" Garner asked.

"Until their ground team figures out their tracker isn't talking to them anymore and resets it manually. Could be twenty minutes. Could be five."

"Then let's not count on it," Garner said.

"Mexican helicopters have changed course," Delaney added. "They're vectoring toward the site now."

"Let them," Renn said. "By the time they arrive, all they'll find is Prometheus explaining why they're in Mexican territory with heavy weapons."

Delaney couldn't help it. "That's going to be an interesting conversation."

They flew north for thirty minutes before Renn gave new coordinates. "Rendezvous point. Mother ship will be waiting."

The location was another section of empty desert, back on the American side of the border. As they approached, a massive cigar-shaped craft materialized seemingly out of nothing, the cloaking technology dropping away to reveal the enormous vessel.

Garner brought them to a hover fifty yards from the ship. He did not mention what the engines had been doing for the last half hour, but Delaney had been watching the fuel display.

A portal opened on the ship's side, and a platform extended.

"Lower the craft onto the platform," Renn instructed.

Delaney carefully released the cargo hooks once the damaged Tic Tac was stable on the platform. It retracted, and the Gray alien pilot stood, moving toward the crew door.

Renn opened it, and warm desert air rushed in. The Gray paused at the threshold, its hand reaching out to touch Renn's shoulder. A kind of silent communication that Delaney had witnessed before.

Then the being stepped carefully onto a smaller platform that had extended from the mother ship. It retracted, the portal closed, and the massive craft faded from view.

"Package delivered," Garner said. "Now let's talk about fuel."

Delaney pulled up the reserve display. The number was not good. The damaged anti-gravity field had cost them badly on burn rate, more than he could have projected without knowing how far the compensation system had failed. He ran the calculation twice before he said it aloud.

"We're not forty minutes past our margin. We're at ninety. McClellan is possible, but we need a straight line and no headwinds."

"Give me the altitude," Garner said.

"Twenty-one thousand. Best cruise burn at this weight."

Garner was already climbing. Delaney watched him work the throttle settings with a precision that had nothing casual about it. Every adjustment was deliberate. He was not flying the aircraft. He was managing it.

"There's a fifteen-knot tailwind out of the northwest at that altitude," Delaney said, pulling the weather data. "That buys us something."

"How much?"

"Maybe the difference between making it and not."

Neither of them said anything else about fuel for the next two hours.

Renn had not spoken since the mother ship departed. She was in one of the rear crew seats with her eyes closed and her hands flat on her knees. Garner glanced back once. Delaney knew what he was checking.

She was still breathing normally, but the color had not come back to her face, and she had not moved in a long time.

"Director." Garner kept his voice even. "You with us?"

"Yes," she said, without opening her eyes. "Give me an hour."

Garner looked at Delaney. Delaney looked at the fuel gauge.

They landed at McClellan Airport with less in the tanks than anyone said out loud. The engines spooled down, and Garner sat with his hands in his lap for a moment before he reached for the checklist.

"I need a drink," Delaney said.

Garner said nothing. He was still looking at the fuel numbers.

Renn unstrapped slowly. "Get some rest. We refuel, file a legitimate flight plan for S-3, and depart at first light. This mission never happened."

"What mission?" Garner asked, with a slight grin that didn't quite reach his eyes.

As Delaney climbed out of the cockpit, he glanced back at the rear crew seats where the injured Gray had been. There was no evidence that anyone had been there. No blood, no marks, nothing.

Just another ghost flight with cargo that officially didn't exist, rescued from a crash that never happened, and delivered to a ship that wasn't there.

Delaney noticed he hadn't thought to check whether there was blood. He just looked for cargo and found none. That was probably what adapting felt like.

Chapter Thirteen

Immaculate Deception

In the Ready Room, Lieutenant Mark Delaney waited impatiently for the coffeemaker to finish. He noticed Director Renn studying a video playing on the wall-mounted display screen.

She looked over and called, "Lieutenant, you'll want to see this."

The coffee machine stopped. "Be right there," he replied as he filled his cup.

On the screen, what appeared to be a cellphone video showed a small-town church. What got his attention was a translucent sphere surrounding a dark cube, hovering in the air above the church.

"Millfield, Kansas," Renn said. "The video went viral early this morning."

Captain Garner appeared in the doorway. "What are we looking at?"

"Social media is convinced it's either the Second Coming or an alien invasion."

Garner crossed his arms. "Okay, so what is it really?"

"Not what they think it is. It's a fake. A good one, but a fake."

"Any idea who might be responsible?" Delaney asked.

Garner uncrossed his arms. "My guess would be Prometheus Applied Sciences. We've had suspicions General Briggs has been providing access to recovered alien wrecks. Remote holographic projection wouldn't be a stretch."

"Good guess." Renn pulled up another screen. "Prometheus has been positioning itself as the solution to extraterrestrial threats. Detection arrays, threat assessment protocols and weapons systems."

Delaney set down his coffee mug on a nearby table. "Create the problem and sell the solution."

"Exactly." The director turned to face them. "They stage UFO events, social media amplifies the panic, and suddenly every congressman with a military base in their district is demanding alien defense capabilities, and Prometheus is the only contractor claiming to have the expertise."

Captain Garner stepped closer to the text on the screen. "So we scramble Pandora, track down their projection system, and shut it down."

Renn shook her head. "Won't work. They probably packed up and moved on to another location. It could be anywhere. We would be chasing shadows."

"Then what's the plan?"

Renn looked at Delaney. "This is your wheelhouse, Lieutenant. We need to see inside their network to get ahead of them."

Delaney spoke softly. "Director, my cyber ops days ..."

"You were on the inside blocking the doors. I also know you could ghost through SUBPAC's firewall without leaving a fingerprint."

The lieutenant's response was something between a question mark and a guilty smile.

"I'll need access to the secure terminal," he said finally.

Renn nodded. "You'll have whatever you need."

***

The S-3 secure communications room occupied a separate level above the crew quarters. Delaney sat at a desk surrounded by three monitors and a rack of computer servers.

He started with a search of public records. If Prometheus was responsible, that's where the trail would begin.

Based in Virginia, Prometheus Applied Sciences held seventeen Department of Defense contracts with a total value north of two billion dollars. Corporate officers, board members, lobbying expenditures, all documented and legal.

To satisfy his suspicions, he dug deeper into supply chain data, real estate transactions, some filtered through shell companies. He looked for locations with high-power consumption and found a facility in New Mexico drawing megawatts, operated by a subsidiary identified as Revelation Technologies, LLC.

"Revelation," Delaney muttered. "Not exactly subtle, are they?"

Through a public NASA connection, he brought up a satellite image ... an isolated warehouse complex, miles away from the nearest town, evidence of recent construction, with a heavy security perimeter: the kind of place that did not invite visitors.

The hard part was next.

Delaney pulled a thumb drive from his pocket. On it was a program he had toyed with six years back, designed for just this kind of investigation. He hesitated. Eleven years ago, he had raised his right hand and sworn an oath, not to outcomes, but to process. To lawful orders. To the chain of command his father had served inside for twenty-three years, even when the real work had to be done in the shadows. What he was about to do had no authorization, no legal cover, and no clean explanation if it unraveled. He wasn't protecting the system. He was breaking into one. Getting caught could expose the entire Mogul operation, and the one doing the exposing would be him.

Then he thought about the alternative, and his fingers moved with purpose.

His social engineering attack was precise. With his software file, he spoofed credentials from Prometheus' own IT department, injected a system email about a security audit, and waited for someone to click the embedded link. It took less than twenty minutes for a response.

"Come on!" Delaney whispered. "Talk to me!"

Eventually, the first firewall opened. The security was good. Military-grade encryption, compartmentalized access, and an intrusion detection system that would make most hackers pack up and leave. But Delaney wasn't most hackers. The Navy had trained him to penetrate networks with nation-states.

He carefully mapped out the infrastructure, probing for weaknesses until he found one: a legacy server that had not been updated in eight months. He was in.

One routing path traced through an experimental relay at Area 51, listed under Advanced Research Programs as Site Seven, under a Dr. Victor Harmon. It dead-ended well away from anything Prometheus-related, government infrastructure with no apparent connection to what he was looking for. He noted the node and moved on.

Internal communication spread across his screen: project files, financial records, deployment schedules.

And there it was: Project Revelation.

Delaney downloaded everything. There were technical schematics for the holographic display projector. It was very sophisticated, likely using principles learned from recovered alien technology, and manufactured terrestrially.

Even more surprising were the financial records showing payments to General Briggs, routed through offshore accounts.

There was also a street address in Sedona, Arizona.

Delaney dug further. There were communications with congressional staffers, members of the defense appropriations committee, and think tank analysts. This went beyond selling weapons. Prometheus was attempting to reshape security policy, to convince the government that extraterrestrial defense needed to be a budget priority.

He kept digging, pulling financial data from a subdirectory labeled CONGRESSIONAL OUTREACH. The files downloaded smoothly, filling his local cache with evidence.

Until the download speed changed.

Delaney's attention was drawn to the network monitor in the corner of his screen. Bandwidth dropped by forty percent in the last thirty seconds. Not a gradual decline, but a deliberate throttle.

He opened a second terminal window and ran a packet trace. His connection was being routed through additional nodes he had not specified. Someone had inserted monitoring stations into his data stream.

"Smart," he muttered.

He did not get cut off, and he had not triggered any alarms. Not yet, anyway. They were just watching, tracing, buying time to identify his location while keeping him connected and thinking he was still invisible.

Delaney checked his connection logs. He discovered an active trace program, elegantly hidden inside what looked like routine network maintenance traffic. It had already narrowed his location to North America. It was only a matter of time, perhaps less than a minute, before they would have his facility, and after that they would pinpoint his terminal. He knew the game well.

He executed his exit protocol. Ghost packets flooded false trails. Randomized routing through international servers and connection termination protocols would scrub his presence from their logs.

Delaney had what he needed without leaving a trace.

***

Director Renn and Captain Garner filtered through the printed documents spread across the briefing table. Delaney took his time laying out the evidence, all of it physical, none of it traceable. Old school, in the best possible sense.

Renn cautioned, "If we move too early with an investigation, Prometheus will just lawyer up and buy time in litigation for years. Meanwhile, they keep operating."

"Sedona in three days," Delaney reminded. "Another UFO hotspot, maximum media attention, and coverage. This one will be much bigger."

Russ Garner straightened. "We scramble Pandora and intercept their deployment team before ..."

"No." Renn's voice was flat and stern. "We stop one operation, they'll just set up another one in a different location, that time being more careful. We need to cut off the head."

Delaney had been thinking about a strategy for the past hour. "We don't go to the media, we go to the Inspector General's office. Let the Pentagon's internal watchdogs do what they do best."

"They'll bury it," Garner protested.

"Not if we give them something they can't ignore." Delaney pulled a document from under the pile. "Prometheus's alien defense weapons are rebranded conventional arms with a big markup. That's not conspiracy theory territory, it's fraud. It's theft of taxpayer money. The IG's office will tear them apart."

Pointing at the sheet in Mark's hand, Garner said, "The evidence should be enough for an indictment. And Briggs is done at the same time."

Renn studied the papers a few at a time. "And what if Prometheus somehow comes after us before the investigation gains traction?"

"A dead man's switch tied to a dozen press inboxes and oversight committees." Delaney met her eyes. "If Prometheus tries to fake another event, everything goes public. Every news outlet, every congressional office, every watchdog group. They make a move in retaliation, they destroy themselves."

Garner looked at Director Renn. "This could blow back on us. Unauthorized cyber intrusion ..."

"That's if they ever suspect we're involved, which I doubt they will," Delaney assured him.

Renn was quiet for a moment, weighing the risks.

"I'm aware. I'm also aware that Delaney just handed us the ability to stop a domestic terrorist operation masquerading as a defense contractor." She turned to Mark. "Send the package to the IG. Anonymous, untraceable. You know how."

Delaney nodded.

Director Renn said, "Thank you."

***

Three days later, Delaney sat in the Ready Room with a fresh cup of coffee, monitoring news feeds on his tablet and waiting. Captain Garner was relaxing in a chair, cleaning his flight goggles.

"Anything yet?" he asked.

"If you mean Sedona, nothing so far," Delaney answered. "No mysterious lights, no panicked crowds. Just tourists taking pictures of red rocks."

As he said that, his phone buzzed with a news alert.

> "PENTAGON SUSPENDS CONTRACTS WITH PROMETHEUS APPLIED SCIENCES PENDING INVESTIGATION."

Then another alert:

> "ARMY MAJOR GENERAL BRIGGS ANNOUNCES RETIREMENT."

Garner sat up. "Well, isn't that interesting!"

Director Renn heard the phone buzz and came out of her office at the other end of the room. She glanced at Mark's phone screen.

"The IG's office moved faster than I expected. I'm guessing they've already frozen Prometheus's assets pending investigation of fraud."

"How long until they're completely shut down?" Delaney wondered.

"Months, maybe years for the full prosecution," Renn responded. "But their operation is effectively over. No more fake alien visitations."

Delaney was sipping his coffee when Renn said quietly, "You had to cross some lines."

Delaney set down his cup. "My father spent twenty-three years navigating the rules. I'm just hoping he'd understand why I had to break them." He looked up. "I keep telling myself the outcome justified it. I'm not sure he would have agreed." He picked the cup back up. "But I'd do it again."

Delaney refreshed the news feed. The story was spreading: whispers of corruption, fraudulent contracts, manufactured threats. It would take time for the full story to emerge, but at this point it was unstoppable.

Garner got up to leave. "You OK?" he asked Mark.

"Yeah. I was afraid it wouldn't work and blow up in my face. Worse, it could have shut down Project Mogul. And then what? I hate to think about that, and not just about our jobs."

"I know what you mean. Really. You took a chance, but for all the right reasons nobody will ever know."

He smiled and tapped the door frame twice as he was leaving.

Chapter Fourteen

Nimitz Intervention

Exactly three months after the Sonoran operation, the klaxon tore through the pre-dawn calm in the Ready Room. Director Kaela Renn was moving by the time it sounded again, her platinum hair reflecting the red emergency lights as tactical displays lit up the room.

"Multiple gravimetric anomalies detected," the automated voice announced. "Designation: Gray signatures. Location: Pacific Ocean, sector seven-nine-three. Navy assets in active pursuit."

Captain Garner zipped up his flight suit, hands moving quickly. "How many?"

"Four contacts." Renn's hands moved across the display screen controls, pulling up satellite feeds. Thermal imaging flooded the screen: the USS Nimitz carrier group, four blurs darting between ships. "Tic-Tac configuration. They're running circles around the battle group."

Delaney burst in, tablet in hand, hair still wet from a rushed shower. "Director, we've got a problem. I'm seeing encrypted Space Command chatter from the Pinckney. They've armed something called Project Lancer. Looks like a directed-energy weapon."

Renn's jaw tightened. She'd pictured this exact mess before, some admiral playing cowboy, ready to pull the trigger and deal with the fallout later.

"Can you stop them?" she asked.

“Not in time.” Delaney’s hands flew across his tablet. “They’re already in the firing sequence. Wait ...” He froze, color draining from his face. “Director, they just fired.”

The tactical display exploded with white light as the energy discharge bloomed across the screen. When the light faded, three of the Gray signatures shot off at speeds that didn’t seem possible. The fourth tumbled, its gravimetric signature flickering wildly.

“It’s going down,” Garner said, tracking the wounded craft as it fell. “San Clemente Island. North shore, looks like.”

Renn was already heading for the hangar. “Spin up Pandora 2. Lieutenant, stall the destroyer’s recovery teams. Keep them off our backs.”

“On it.” Delaney began typing before she finished.

“Captain Garner, how fast can you get us there?”

Garner checked his watch. “We could break ground and be on station in just over an hour. But Director ...” He looked her in the eye. “Navy’s going to have birds in the air as soon as there’s daylight. That gives us under two hours.”

“Then we’re gone in one.”

Pandora 2 roared across the Pacific, slicing through the night at its maximum 320 miles an hour, twin Rolls-Royce AE 1107F turboshaft engines screaming. Inside, red lights threw jagged shadows across Garner’s face as he kept the V-280 skimming two hundred feet above the waves, just low enough to dodge the Navy’s radar.

Delaney, riding shotgun, juggled three screens: one infiltrating the destroyer’s systems, another watching Pandora 2‘s sensors, and a third tracking Navy air assets.

“Okay, I’m in their network,” he said, voice tight. “Their MH-60S is already getting preflight checks. Pilot, copilot, four-man boarding team, everyone suiting up.”

“Can you stop the launch?” Renn called from behind. Through the windscreen, San Clemente Island was just a dark smudge on the horizon.

"Not without setting off alarms. But I can give them some equipment trouble." Delaney's fingers moved across the haptic keys. "Injecting fake diagnostics. Hydraulic pressure warnings, rotor imbalance alert. Nothing dangerous, just enough to ground them for a bit. That should buy us thirty, maybe thirty-five minutes."

"Do it."

Garner banked north, hugging the rocky coast. "Director, GAD's got the target. Sending coordinates now."

Renn glanced at her tablet. The Gravimetric Anomaly Detector had locked onto the Gray propulsion signature, even damaged and powered down. The crash site was a mile inland, buried in a rugged ravine thick with brush and stone.

"No place to land," Garner said, eyeing the ground. "I'll have to hold a hover while you fast-rope down."

"I'm reading residual energy," Delaney added. "Craft's still got power. Could be dangerous."

Renn stood, grabbing her tactical vest. "Someone might still be alive." She clipped a medical kit to her belt, grabbed a scanner and an emergency beacon. "Lieutenant, keep an eye on Navy comms. Captain, get me over that site."

"Copy." Garner's voice was calm as he shifted Pandora 2 into helicopter mode, rotors swinging to vertical as the aircraft slowed to a hover. "Silence Mode on."

The engines faded from a roar to a hush, as if the world were holding its breath.

Garner eased the aircraft south toward the canyon. On the approach the GAD had looked clean, walls wide enough for a comfortable hover with room to spare. In practice, the canyon was not what it had looked like from altitude.

The east wall was fifteen feet closer than the terrain model showed. He caught it in the rotor wash before he saw it on any display: the distinctive push-back of air compressing between the blade tips and rock. He was already too far into the canyon to pull out cleanly, and the crash site was directly below.

"Canyon's tighter than the GAD had it," he said, keeping his voice level. "East wall is a problem. I need to reposition."

He moved the aircraft thirty feet west and held it there, reading the new position through the collective. The rotor clearance was workable but not comfortable. It also put him offset from the vertical center of the crash site, which meant any hoist cable going straight down from the side door would hit the canyon floor at an angle.

He would deal with that when Renn needed to come back up.

"Not much room to work with," he said. "Going to be slower than planned. Stay on comms."

"Got it." Renn slid the side door open. The hoist was already rigged on the port arm. Cold Pacific air slapped her face as she clipped the fast-rope to the anchor overhead and kicked it out. She watched it snake down into the dark. "Going down."

She dropped fast, boots hitting the rocks in twenty seconds. Renn unclipped and moved toward the crash site, yanking night-vision goggles over her eyes. The world snapped to a grainy green.

The Tic-Tac craft was jammed into the hillside, its shell cracked and scorched. Smaller than she'd pictured, maybe fifteen feet, smooth and oblong. The impact had ripped one side wide open. Inside, a faint glow pulsed along the walls, almost alive.

At the sight, a stabbing pain.

It wasn't just pain. It was a mind screaming into hers that knocked her sideways, and she gripped the rock to stay upright. She'd never tried to connect with a Gray like this before. The idea of their minds touching hers made her shudder.

But someone was alive in that wreck.

She forced herself forward, climbing over smoking debris to the torn hull. Inside, two alien bodies were slumped in what looked like acceleration couches. One was gone; a crushed skull left no doubt. The other was still respirating, barely. Shallow, rapid.

Renn knelt next to the survivor, holding her hand just above its face. She felt its mind flicker, close to going out.

We meant no harm. The thought was weak, broken. *Just medical observation. Watching our children.*

"Your children?" Renn whispered, catching herself. She needed to focus. "I'm here to help. Let's get you out."

The fire. The fire from the sky-vessel. They attacked us.

"I know. We're not with them. We're ..." She paused. What were they, really? "We're here to help."

Delaney's voice cut in over comms, quieter than she would have liked. "Director, we have a problem. Their diagnostics cleared. Whatever I injected, their crew chief found it and ran a manual override. The MH-60S is ready for launch."

"How long?" Renn asked, not taking her hand away from the alien.

"Seven minutes. Maybe eight."

He sat back from the panel and looked at his options. He could inject a second layer of faults deeper into the helicopter's system, but that risked triggering a security audit on the aircraft's integrity that would flag external intrusion. The Nimitz group would know their network had been penetrated. That was a line he didn't want to cross.

The second option was to let the helicopter launch and find another way to slow it en route. He didn't love that either.

He chose a third option.

He moved up the network from the destroyer to the carrier's air traffic control system, which was less hardened and less monitored at this hour. Inside the ATC database, he located the airspace management module and inserted a no-fly buffer around a two-mile radius of the crash site coordinates, flagged as a temporary radiological contamination zone. He gave it a false originating authority: Naval Reactors, Incident Response Division. The flag would not survive scrutiny, but scrutiny took time, and the on-duty ATC watch officer would hold all air assets until someone senior enough to override it could be reached.

"I've got them," he said. "I put a radiological no-fly flag over the site through their own ATC. It'll collapse when someone calls Naval Reactors and finds out they never issued it. Ten minutes, maybe twelve."

Garner's voice came over the channel: "That's what we needed."

"Don't thank me yet. Clock's running."

Back in the wreck, the Gray's breathing had steadied slightly. The flicker of its mind had not gone out. But it was not transmitting, not yet. It was watching.

Renn felt the scrutiny of it, a careful, methodical presence pressing at the edges of her consciousness. Not the weak desperate thing from a moment ago. Something more deliberate. It was reading her.

What are you?

Not a question. A test.

"I'm human," she said, and felt the alien's skepticism even before the words were out.

Not only. We can see the difference. We have watched its kind before.

Renn went still. She had spent her entire career managing exactly this gap, the space between what she was and what her file said she was. She had learned to hold it carefully, the way you carry something fragile in a crowd, and she had never set it down deliberately.

The Gray would not transmit to a human observer. Its medical data, the genetic records, the documentation of its program, all of it was locked behind a recognition threshold. It was testing whether she was what she appeared to be, or whether she was something it could trust with what it carried.

"Director." Garner's voice in her earpiece. "I'm reading elevated energy levels in that craft. Whatever's keeping it powered is becoming unstable. You need to move."

"One minute," she said.

She made the decision and did what she had never done deliberately. She lowered every barrier she had ever built, all the way down, and let the alien read what was underneath.

The contact was immediate and total. The Gray was inside her memories before she finished the breath: her father's pale eyes in a photograph she had studied her entire life, the medical scans from her first Project Mogul evaluation that the senior officer had looked at twice before filing without comment, the moment three years into her directorship when she had first understood what she was looking at when she looked in the mirror. It moved through all of it quickly and without apology. Her feelings about what it found didn't interest it. It was only interested in whether the finding was genuine.

It was.

You carry the marker. The recognition settled through the connection like a key turning. *Bridge generation. Not ours. But known to us.*

Then it opened.

The memories came in a flood. Not hers. The alien's: ships hovering above carriers at night, systematic crew scans from orbit, a young sailor on a flight deck with eyes a shade too wide and hands that were subtly, wrongly proportioned. Another with a skull architecture that no human baseline quite explained. Hybrids. The descendants of old contact programs, integrated into the fleet, living as humans, not knowing the truth of what they carried. The Grays had been tracking them for decades, monitoring their health, confirming their integration, documenting the program's reach generation by generation.

We have our children. You are not one of them. But the marker is the same. Someone else found the same door.

And then the pain. Grief that was not hers, bigger than one being, as if the loss of the pilot in the other couch tore through a network of minds that extended far beyond this canyon.

"I'm sorry," she said. Not for the first time. The words felt smaller than what she meant.

My partner. Tell me.

She glanced at the dead Gray, then back. She could lie. Maybe she should.

"I'm sorry," she said again. "They didn't make it."

The grief hit her a second time, as raw as the first.

"Director." Delaney's voice in her ear, tight. "The radiological flag just got escalated. Someone senior is on the phone to Naval Reactors right now. We have maybe four minutes before that no-fly clears."

Renn made her call. She pressed her hand to the Gray's skull and held the connection open as the alien's consciousness began to dim.

The vessel core. They must retrieve the vessel core. Our kinship. The medical data. All of it is recorded.

“I’ll find it. But you need to let go now. Your people are waiting outside.”

The Gray’s large black eyes fixed on her face. She felt it truly seeing her, not the uniform, not the human surface, but the thing underneath that it had recognized. A flicker of something crossed its dying mind. Not quite surprise. Closer to recognition confirmed.

And then it was gone. The consciousness simply ceased, like a switch thrown. Renn jerked her hand back and stayed on her knees for a moment, breathing hard. The body lay still. Just another piece of wreckage now.

“Director?” Garner’s voice was sharp. “Energy levels are climbing. You need to be out of that craft.”

Renn looked around the interior. Her eyes settled on a sphere embedded in the bulkhead, pulsing with faint light. She pried it free. It was not much larger than a peach, warm and slightly yielding, like organic tissue.

“I’ve got the core,” she said. “I need the hoist.”

“Copy.” A pause. “Delaney, you have the aircraft. Hold this hover.”

“I have the aircraft,” Delaney confirmed, hands already on the controls.

Through the torn hull above her, she heard Garner moving aft through Pandora 2‘s cabin passage toward the side door. Thirty seconds later the hoist cable dropped into the canyon, the rescue strop swinging at the end.

It was not directly above her.

Because of the repositioned hover, the cable came down at an angle, maybe fifteen degrees off vertical, the strop hanging toward the far wall of the canyon rather than straight down to the crash site floor. Getting to it meant crossing four feet of unstable debris.

She crossed it, secured the sphere in her vest, and reached for the strop. Getting it over her head and under her arms with a medical kit on her belt took longer than it should have. She cinched it tight and clicked the safety latch.

“On,” she said.

The cable took her weight. The angle immediately pulled her toward the canyon wall, the physics of an off-axis load swinging her out from the vertical. She put a hand up to fend off the rock face as the hoist motor lifted her past the torn hull edge.

In the cockpit, Delaney felt the aircraft yaw slightly as the angled load shifted Pandora 2's trim. He corrected, but the correction put him back into the rotor clearance problem on the east wall. He split the difference and held it, watching the hoist camera feed with both hands on the controls and his jaw set.

Above the canyon, Garner was working the hoist manually, compensating for the swing with short, controlled bursts rather than a steady pull. The cable came up in jerks. Each jerk changed the pendulum angle. He read the physics of it and timed his inputs to reduce the swing rather than fight it.

It took longer than a straight lift. The canyon walls slid past. The sky above was gray-pink at the edges.

When the opening of Pandora 2's side door came level, Garner reached out and pulled her in by the harness.

She sat on the floor with her back against the bulkhead. She did not move for several seconds. The contact with the dying Gray had not simply ended when she broke it. She could still feel the edges of it, raw and open the way a wound is open before the body registers pain. Her hands were shaking, and she pressed them flat against the floor to keep it from showing.

"Delaney, what's our status?" she said when she could.

"Radiological flag just cleared. Their MH-60S is released for flight. Call it three minutes before they're airborne."

Garner was already moving back through the cabin passage to the cockpit. "I need you in a seat with a harness," he called over his shoulder. "Now."

He dropped into the left seat and took the controls from Delaney. The rotors tilted as Pandora 2 surged away from the crash site.

"Where's that other Gray signature?" Garner asked.

Delaney checked his display. "Still holding offshore. Wait. It's moving. Coming toward us."

Through the windscreen, they saw it: a luminous disc rising from the dark ocean, water streaming off its surface. It moved with impossible grace, matching Pandora 2's course and speed, pacing them just off the port side.

Renn moved to the window, the data sphere clutched against her chest. She could feel it: a consciousness aboard that craft, probing gently at her mind. She lowered her barriers slightly, projecting intent rather than words.

Your crew is dead. I have their medical data. I'm sorry.

The disc wobbled slightly, as if its pilot had been struck.

Why do you help us?

Because someone had to.

A pause. Then the disc pulled ahead, accelerating to a speed Pandora 2 could not hope to match. But before it disappeared over the horizon, she felt one last thought touch her mind: gratitude.

And then it was gone, leaving only the dark Pacific and the approaching dawn.

"Navy helo is three minutes out," Delaney reported as they dropped back down to wave-top height. "We're clear."

Garner let out a slow breath. "We burned more on the deck than I'd like, but we have enough to get home. Where to, Director?"

Renn sat heavily in the crew seat, staring at the sphere in her hands. The data scrolling across her mind revealed a map of hidden lives, hybrids tucked into human families across the globe, biological sleepers waiting for a call they might never hear. Information that could shatter families, end careers, or worse, be weaponized by factions within the government who saw hybrids as threats rather than bridge species.

"Take us home," she said quietly. "And nobody mentions this in the after-action report. Nobody."

"Director?" Delaney turned in his seat. "What did you find down there?"

She met his eyes, saw the curiosity there, and made a decision. Some truths had to be protected, even from good people.

"Two dead Grays and a crashed ship," she said. "Nothing more."

The lie tasted bitter. But after decades of living one, what was one more?

As San Clemente Island disappeared behind them and the sun painted the eastern sky pink and gold, Director Kaela Renn held the sphere tighter and wondered if the Grays had the right idea after all. Maybe the only way to survive in a hostile universe was to seed it quietly, generation by generation, until the definition of human became too blurred to matter.

Garner glanced back. "What do we do with it? The sphere?"

Renn's grip tightened. "Secure vault. No analysis, no reports. Some things are safer buried."

"And if someone asks?"

"Two dead Grays and salvaged tech," she said. "If Command gets hold of this, they'll treat it as a threat. We bury it to maintain the balance."

Maybe that was the only path to peace. Or maybe it was just another form of invasion, patient and inexorable. She didn't have an answer. She only knew that somewhere aboard the USS Nimitz, sailors with slightly unusual bone structure were beginning their morning shifts, unaware that they carried alien DNA, unaware that they'd just been orphaned by a weapon they'd never see.

The sun rose higher. Through the windscreen, the Pacific turned from black to gray to a flat, hard blue. Renn did not look at it. She kept her eyes on the sphere in her lap, both hands around it, and said nothing for the rest of the flight home.

Chapter Fifteen

Shadows Over Yuma

Director Kaela Renn had been at her desk since 0400. The after-action report was filed and transmitted; two sentences that covered what had happened off San Clemente without covering any of it. She had not slept. The sphere was in the vault. The sphere's contents were not.

Beyond her door, the Ready Room was quiet. Garner and Delaney had gone to their quarters hours earlier.

As Director Renn closed her eyes, a sharp beep from the secure terminal snapped her awake. Through the door in the Ready Room, a red alert light was flashing. The secure terminal screen flashed the word ALERT, the message from Project Mogul Command locked behind top-secret biometric protocols.

Director Renn pressed her hand onto the reader, the faint green glow of the scanner tracing the ridges of her palm. At the same time, a light pulse swept across her iris. The machine accepted her presence with a muted chime, and the encoded message spread across the display.

PROJECT MOGUL PRIORITY ALERT

Source: Military Command, Southwest Theater

Incident: Crashed UAP, restricted zone adjacent to Barry Goldwater Range, Yuma, AZ

Target Coordinates: 32.68N, 113.52W

Detail: Military Presence. Directed energy / laser fire reported on perimeter.

Mission Objective: Containment. Prevent escalation.

Renn leaned back in her chair, her eyes narrowing. The words carried weight, but her instincts whispered warnings. She had learned to trust her instincts. Tonight, the whisper was sharp and cold. Something about this felt wrong. Crashes happened, but laser fire holding back troops? That was not alien behavior. That was human tactics.

She keyed the intercom: "Delaney, Garner: Ready Room."

Lieutenant Delaney arrived first, his dark hair damp from a recent shower. Captain Russ Garner followed, steady and deliberate, his crewcut framing a face carved by years of responding to risk.

Renn gestured to the now-quieted terminal screen. "Command reports a downed alien craft near Yuma. Troops claim they are being held back by laser fire. Our orders are containment. They didn't say how."

Garner frowned and brushed his fingers across the side of his head. "Laser fire? That's not standard for aliens. Defensive fields, yes. But direct energy projection? Doesn't fit."

Delaney crossed his arms in agreement.

Renn's gaze lingered on the captain. "I share your suspicion." She tapped the console. "We'll investigate, but we need to be sure we're not walking into a snare. Pandora 2 prepped?"

"Ten minutes," Garner responded.

The huge mountain hangar doors rumbled open as the ground crew towed Pandora 2 out into the desert night, silhouetting its sleek tiltrotor frame against the stars.

In the cockpit, Garner adjusted the cyclic controller, his hands moving with practiced confidence. Delaney checked the Tactical Data Core, watching the artificial intelligence diagnostic sweep across the systems. Then the diagnostic stalled. A phantom background process had attached itself to their telemetry feed and was consuming thirty percent of his processing power. He had to manually partition the core just to get the mission-critical systems online.

"Something's piggybacking on our telemetry," he muttered, his fingers working across the tablet as he tried to isolate the intrusive code. He could see it, but he couldn't remove it cleanly without risking the core entirely. He quarantined it and moved on.

The processing loss was going to be a problem. Pandora 2's terrain-following system ran off the same computational budget, and thirty percent short was not a negligible loss when flying at low altitude in unfamiliar high desert.

Renn strapped into the rear crew seat, her posture rigid. "Two miles short of the target coordinates. We go in low to stay off the radar. Then we land and observe. No direct approach." She leaned forward between the seats and handed Delaney a sheet with the coordinates.

Garner shouted, "Clear!" as the twin engines came to life. Pandora 2 lifted smoothly, rising above the desert floor before banking south. The night stretched wide and empty, broken only by the glow of distant range lights.

***

The foothills came up fast on the approach, and Garner knew immediately that the terrain-following was not going to carry him through it.

The system's display was stuttering, feeding him altitude returns half a second behind where the aircraft actually was. At five hundred feet over open desert, it might not matter. At two hundred feet, threading between ridgelines in unfamiliar terrain at night, half a second was the difference between a concealed landing and a rotor strike.

He went off the display entirely.

What he had instead was fifteen years of reading landscape from a cockpit: the way a ridgeline's shadow pools in the dip before the rock face rises, the color shift in the ground texture that signals loose alluvial fan dropping into a wash, the particular way desert air moves over a confined space and pushes back against the rotors when the walls are close. He felt all of it through his hands and adjusted for it without naming what he was doing.

Delaney said nothing. He had the presence of mind to keep the sensor feeds quiet and let Garner work.

The aircraft settled into a natural bowl between two low ridges, screened from the target coordinates by three hundred yards of rising ground. It was not where the system would have put them. It was better.

Garner reduced power and let the rotors spool down to a low idle. "We're in," he said, his voice even.

Delaney released a breath he had been holding for two minutes. "Good approach."

"Terrain-following was down. I just flew it."

Delaney's attention had already moved back to the processing problem. The phantom code was still sitting in the quarantine partition, and something about its structure was bothering him in a way he hadn't had time to examine on the approach. He filed it and watched the screens.

Renn unbuckled and looked at Garner. "Open the hatch."

Garner released his harness and leaned forward. Renn braced a hand on the seat frame, letting it take some of her weight as she slid past to reach the doorway. Grabbing the handrail, she lowered her legs to find the recessed footrails below the cockpit, then lowered herself to the desert floor.

Renn marched into the open desert until she was two hundred yards from the aircraft, beyond the rotor noise, beyond the heat signature of the engines. The ground was flat and pale under the moon.

She stopped and stood still.

What she was about to do, she had not done deliberately before. She had felt the edge during other contacts, the way her hybrid nature registered differently to alien sensor systems, not quite human, not quite Nordic, something that occupied its own frequency. She had always kept that quality contained. It was, in practical terms, camouflage. Projecting it outward was the opposite of containment. It was the equivalent of stepping into the open and removing the cover story entirely.

But the Delta ships needed a reason to come down. A fully human observer standing in the desert would not be one. Delta configuration, triangular, lights at the corners and a brighter source at the center: she had seen the designation in the classified contact registry. Not Grays. Not Nordics. Not Tall Whites. The fourth category, the one the registry listed without species name, only a shape and a behavior pattern and a note that said: no direct communication recorded.

She opened the containment deliberately. It felt, as best she could describe it to herself, like releasing a grip she had held so long she had forgotten it was a grip. The sensation spread outward, and she felt the exposure of it, the same way standing in a lit doorway with darkness behind you makes you aware of how visible you are to anyone in the field outside.

After a few minutes, a shape appeared out of the clouds. It was a large triangle with lights on the corners and a brighter light at the center. It descended silently until it hovered a few hundred yards away and a hundred feet above the ground.

For a long moment, Renn stood in the moonlight and let it read her.

Then she turned back toward Pandora 2. Above her, the delta ship climbed silently and shot skyward, vanishing into the cloud layer.

She reached the aircraft, grabbed the handle, and pulled herself up to the steps and back aboard.

Garner looked at her. She was pale in a way that had nothing to do with the light, and she moved to the crew seat without speaking. Her hands, when she set them on her knees, were not entirely steady.

"You all right?" Garner asked.

"Yes," she said. "Give me a few minutes." She closed her eyes.

Garner and Delaney exchanged a look, then left her to it.

"Watch the target zone," she said quietly, without opening her eyes.

Delaney turned back to his screens. The jamming signal had been building in the background since before they landed, low enough that he had been treating it as interference. Now he looked at it properly.

It was not interference. It was structured.

He ran a countermeasure on the primary frequency and watched the signal shift. It moved to the next available band, not at random but at exactly the rate that would stay ahead of a standard cycling sweep. He ran another countermeasure. It shifted again.

The signal was adaptive. It was responding to what he was doing.

Delaney sat back from the panel. Someone had built this knowing exactly how the MSSA cycled its countermeasures. The frequency response pattern was not a coincidence or a lucky design. It was tailored. Whoever wrote the jamming algorithm had either accessed Pandora 2's sensor specifications or had worked from them directly.

"We have a problem," he said.

Garner looked over.

"The jammer is adaptive. It knows our countermeasure sequence." Delaney paused. "Somebody built this for us specifically."

Garner's jaw tightened. "That's the intelligence failure."

"Right." Delaney looked at his options. He could keep cycling countermeasures and lose the cat-and-mouse eventually, because the algorithm had the initiative. Or he could go manual on all sensors and deny the jammer anything to respond to. It was a clean decision with an ugly consequence: several minutes of no sensor picture, no tracking, no MSSA output. They would be operationally blind.

That was when the trap was supposed to close.

He went manual.

"Sensors are dark," he said. "I'm off all active systems. If there's something moving toward us right now, I won't see it for the next three to four minutes."

"Understood," Garner said. He moved his hand to the power controls and kept it there.

The screens went quiet. Outside the cockpit, the desert was still. Delaney counted seconds and watched the dark. Renn had not moved from the crew seat behind them.

Three minutes and forty seconds. He brought the sensors back up on manual frequencies, cycling through bands the algorithm had not touched.

The picture rebuilt itself slowly. What it showed was the target coordinates to the southeast, and converging on them from three directions, multiple ground contacts. Military units, moving on the crash site. Whatever window the trap had been designed to exploit had closed without the trap catching anything inside it.

"We're back," Delaney said. "Ground units are at the site. Nothing moved on us."

Garner let out a slow breath and took his hand off the power controls.

***

Meanwhile, at the target location, troops on the ground focused on dark shadows appearing in the clouds above. The shadows soon took the shape of five Delta spacecraft appearing in formation just below the cloud layer.

Below, military units scrambled, turned on floodlights, and raised their weapons. A few soldiers fired, but their rounds failed to penetrate the shimmering glow of the force fields beneath the alien ships. Finally, someone ordered the lights extinguished, and the troops retreated.

***

Back at Pandora 2, Delaney watched the scene resolve on the tracking screens.

As the alien craft lingered, then rose in unison and disappeared into the night sky, Delaney broke the quiet. "Director. What was that about?"

Renn's eyes opened. The color had come back to her face, but only partially. "Somebody on the inside set a trap for us. We just saw them caught in their own deception."

Garner and Delaney exchanged a look. It was more than a glance. It was the quiet recognition that the intelligence failure went somewhere neither of them wanted to follow, yet.

"Let's go home," Renn said. "I have a report to submit to Mogul Command."

Delaney checked the instruments, his fingers steady despite a surge of adrenaline. He gave a firm thumbs-up to Garner. Garner nodded. Delaney opened the red protective covers and flipped the toggle switches in sequence to start the engines. Pandora 2 lifted into the sky as the first pale light of dawn spread across the desert.

The flight north was quiet. Each crew member carried their own thoughts. Delaney replayed the jammer's frequency behavior in his mind. The pattern had been too specific to be accidental. Someone with access to their technical specifications had handed that algorithm to whoever set the trap. That was not an outside breach. That was an inside one.

Garner remained fixed on the flight controls, his jaw tight.

Director Renn sat with her gaze on the horizon. She had left the question of her communication with the Delta ships to conjecture. That was deliberate. Some things were easier to manage if they stayed in the space between what people knew and what they suspected.

***

Pandora 2 descended toward the hidden mountain of S-3. The aircraft settled to a landing; the rotors were folded as the systems powered down, and the ground crew stood by as the pilot and copilot completed the landing checklist. After the crew climbed out, the ground crew towed the aircraft into the hangar.

Back in the Ready Room, Renn addressed the crew, her voice calm but resolute. "Debrief in one hour. Keep your notes precise. Mogul Command will want all the details."

Garner nodded once and said nothing. Delaney hesitated, then spoke quietly. "Director Renn. If there's a mole at Mogul Command, how deep does it go?"

Renn paused at the doorway to her office, framed by the harsh light. "Deep enough that tonight was necessary. But not so deep that we can't cut it out."

She left him with that thought as the office door closed behind her.

Chapter Sixteen

The Mole

Mark Delaney had been awake for nearly nineteen hours, and sleep still refused to come. Renn's voice replayed in his head, quiet but deliberate, deep enough that tonight was necessary.

The Yuma incident hadn't just been a near-miss. Someone had nudged the system at exactly the right moment, with exactly the right information, and watched as the team stepped into the trap.

That kind of precision didn't come from guesswork.

Delaney swung his legs off the bunk and reached for his tablet. At 0241 hours, the S-3 barracks were silent except for the ventilation hum and distant power relays cycling. He activated his emergency diagnostic credentials: temporary, time-limited permissions Renn had authorized after Yuma, and pulled up the incident timeline again.

The false crash alert had arrived through standard Mogul channels. Authentication clean. Formatting perfect. No anomalies in the content itself. If Delaney hadn't been on duty when Pandora 2 diverted, he might never have questioned it.

But the timing still gnawed at him.

The alert had hit S-3 four hours after Renn's encrypted contact with the Nordics regarding the Stolen Thunder operation. Four hours was not a coincidence. It was a window wide enough to prepare, narrow enough to exploit.

Someone had known Renn would act.

Delaney opened a secure terminal on his laptop and began pulling metadata, not content. He did not have permission to decrypt Mogul traffic, and he did not require it. Routing headers, timestamps, relay identifiers, each telling their own story.

Six months of outbound S-3 satellite traffic took longer to assemble than he liked. The first script returned inconsistent results, muddied by routine maintenance reroutes and test traffic. He scrapped it, rewrote the parser, narrowed the dataset.

At 0317 hours, the pattern emerged.

S-3 communications were supposed to uplink to a dedicated military satellite, with a downlink reception at Area 51's primary communications hub. From there, the relay system re-assigned the traffic and forwarded it by hardline to Mogul Command and other cleared recipients.

Under normal conditions, the relay delay averaged eighteen seconds.

The Yuma alert had taken four minutes.

Delaney checked again. He didn't trust the number. He rebuilt the query manually, message by message.

Four minutes.

Three other alerts, less dramatic but oddly well-timed, showed similar delays. Two minutes. Five minutes. Never consistent. Never long enough to trigger automated alarms. The third anomaly looked promising until he traced it to a scheduled satellite handoff. Just maintenance. Just long enough for human intervention.

Delaney leaned back and exhaled slowly, working the logic through his head.

If someone is manipulating traffic, they're not forging Mogul Command messages outright. That would require keys they almost certainly don't have. That means they are targeting the relay point, intercepting messages at Area 51, altering or substituting them, then letting the relay's own signing process make them look legitimate. It would mean the problem isn't inside S-3. It has to be upstream.

Area 51 provided the perfect environment for a hijack, with its deep-seated secrecy and layers of access that made outside auditing impossible. But Delaney knew the base was really just a collection of competing kingdoms, each silo keeping its own secrets from the next.

Delaney pulled up facility maps and cross-referenced them against relay coverage footprints. One site stood out: Site Seven, a research installation northwest of the main complex, officially designated for experimental satellite communications testing. He focused on Site Seven's 'experimental' tag. In his experience, experimental was just a polite word for a place where the standard rulebook didn't apply, a blind spot that could avoid triggering the usual alarms.

Site Seven fell under Advanced Research Programs and Dr. Victor Harmon. Harmon held a seat on the Joint Intelligence Liaison Panel, a quiet advisory body with broad visibility into classified contact programs. Site Seven's experimental relay handled overflow traffic, Harmon's program: advanced signal testing.

Delaney didn't jump to conclusions. He forced himself to rule out alternatives. He reviewed personnel access logs tied to the relay network, flagged overlapping credentials, and chased two dead ends. By the time the sunlight set fire to the horizon, his eyes burned and his hands shook slightly as he drank reheated coffee.

He needed something stronger than inference.

Intercepting satellite traffic left fingerprints, not in the data, but in the signal itself. Every transmitter introduced tiny imperfections: frequency drift, phase noise, and timing jitter. Most systems smoothed them out. But they never vanished entirely.

Delaney configured a controlled test. Using his emergency privileges, he placed S-3's satellite modem into diagnostic capture mode for the next scheduled status transmission. The change was logged, flagged, and time-boxed. He had one shot.

At 0600 hours, S-3 transmitted a routine update.

Delaney captured the raw uplink signal, then waited.

The acknowledgment returned ninety seconds later.

Too long.

He ran the analysis.

The signal was clean, but not right. The frequency stability didn't match Area 51's primary relay profile. Different equipment apparently received, demodulated, and retransmitted the transmission before it entered the relay system.

Someone was in the middle.

That narrowed the field dramatically.

Delaney accessed procurement records tied to Site Seven personnel. Most were unremarkable, routine lab equipment, incremental upgrades.

Harmon's stood out.

Three months earlier, Harmon had authorized a $180,000 acquisition through a defense contractor: a high-gain dish, a wideband receiver, and a software-defined radio suite capable of encrypted signal handling. The justification cited "*advanced signal resilience testing.*"

Technically true. Practically damning.

Still, Delaney needed intent. He built a trap.

The fake operational plan was careful, restrained. No heroics. No imminent action. A plausible reconnaissance extraction in Mexican airspace, seventy-two hours out. Enough to attract attention. Not enough to force a reaction unless someone wanted one.

He transmitted it at 0803 hours.

The relay delay stretched past a minute. Then two.

The forwarded signal bore the same subtle anomalies.

Six hours passed.

At 1421 hours, an urgent alert arrived.

Mexican air defense sensitivity elevated. Recommended postponement of operations near the region.

The message was a masterclass in deception. It sounded perfectly reasonable and conservative, making the lie that much harder to spot.

The RF signature traced back to Area 51's relay, not Mogul Command's transmitters. The message had the right encryption shell and the right signing authority, but the originating node was wrong by four hops. Harmon had routed it through Site Seven's relay and let the relay's own credentials launder it clean.

It would have worked on anyone who stopped at the signature and didn't follow the path back to the source.

That was enough. He flagged one anomaly he hadn't pursued: a second name on the Site Seven procurement authorization, a Dr. Lena Farris, listed as co-approver. Her credentials traced to Advanced Research Programs, the same division as Harmon, a different silo. He added Farris to a separate file and closed the laptop. The Harmon problem was solved. The Farris question was not.

Delaney briefed Renn at 1500 hours, laying out the evidence without embellishment. She listened without interrupting.

When he finished, she nodded once. "We can't use the satellite link."

"No, ma'am."

"And we can't alert Area 51 electronically without tipping him off."

"No, ma'am."

She smiled faintly. "Then we do this the old way."

She reached for a sheet of stationery and a pen. The sealed envelope went directly to Thorne by courier. By the end of the day, Site Seven was silenced. Harmon's access credentials were suspended pending review. His equipment was cataloged. The shutdown happened without a sound, a quiet erasure of credentials and access that left no ripple on the base's daily routine.

That night, Delaney and Garner sat in the ready room sipping beers but said very little. The cleanest victories were the ones that felt like they should have cost more.

"They boxed up his office?" Garner asked.

Delaney nodded. "He thought he was protecting something."

He could see the logic of it now. To a man like Harmon, the secret they were keeping was a fragile thing, and the team at S-3 was a liability: too loud, too physical, and too likely to trip a wire that could never be un-tripped. Harmon likely saw himself as the only one with the discipline to act as a filter. By hijacking the relay, he wasn't just hoarding power; he was acting as a self-appointed gatekeeper, convinced that his bureaucratic silos were the only safe way to manage the truth.

He hadn't been working alone. The Panel gave him cover, institutional access, and at least two names Delaney had now flagged for follow-up. Harmon was the instrument. The Panel was the hand.

Delaney watched the signal monitors return to their predictable, steady hum. He'd spent nineteen hours chasing a digital ghost through the relay, but the most effective weapon against a rogue visionary hadn't been a code or a firewall. It had been a simple slip of paper in a sealed envelope, carried by hand.

He'd found a solution to the immediate crisis, but the night left him with a lingering realization: the most dangerous threats weren't always alien.

Chapter Seventeen

The Long Watch

Director Renn rarely visited the crew quarters recreation area. Her sudden appearance in the doorway caused Captain Garner to look up from the final chapters of a novel by Dale Brown. Lieutenant Delaney glanced away from the terminal screen displaying lines of Python code he'd been debugging.

"Director," Garner said, setting down his reader. "Everything alright?"

Renn stepped inside, her demeanor carrying that particular tension that preceded difficult missions. "We have a situation. Medical transport. High classification, zero visibility."

Delaney saved his work, a packet analysis tool he'd been tinkering with in his spare time. "When?"

"We need to take off in ninety minutes." She moved to the small table between their stations and pulled out a chair. "This one's different. The passenger is being transferred from Wright-Patterson. A Colonel Eriksen, serving under that name currently, though he's been through others. Longer than anyone realizes."

Garner's eyebrows rose slightly. "How much longer?"

"Since 1924."

Delaney's fingers froze over the keyboard. "That's not possible."

"It is if your natural lifespan measures in centuries rather than decades." Renn's fingers drummed once on the table. "He's been rotating through different assignments, different identities, serving under various names. Same person, different paperwork every thirty years or so. The record-keeping was easier before computers."

"What happened?" Garner asked.

"Age finally caught up with him. Or rather, an injury that his physiology can't heal naturally anymore. He collapsed three days ago during a routine training exercise. The base medical staff ran standard diagnostics and found readings that didn't make sense. Before they could dig deeper, someone with the right clearance flagged the case and had him transferred to a secure facility."

"And now he needs treatment that regular military medicine can't provide," Delaney said.

"Area 51 has developed specialized medical protocols. Adapted from decades of research on recovered biological samples." She paused. "This transfer has been in planning for seventy-two hours. It requires an aircraft that can't be tracked, a crew that won't ask questions, and a flight profile that never officially happens."

"Which is why they want to use Pandora instead of a standard medical transport," Garner said.

"Exactly. We file it as a systems test flight. Routine maintenance run. The actual passenger never appears in any manifest."

Delaney minimized his code editor. "What species?"

Renn's eyes met his. "Nordic. Male. More than one hundred years old by our calendar. He's been embedded in U.S. military operations since before World War One. An observation mission that became something more permanent."

"A century of service," Garner said quietly. "That's not observation. It's dedication."

"Or exile," Renn replied. "The distinction isn't always clear." She was quiet for a moment, with the guarded stillness of someone weighing the cost of every word."There was an arrangement. It was a far older, more discreet arrangement than the urban legends about Eisenhower's handshake at Edwards. Eriksen didn't end up in a uniform by accident. He was placed. And the people who placed him made commitments on behalf of this government that no president ever signed and no senator ever read." She met Garner's eyes, then Delaney's. "Which means the commitment was never official, and never ended." She paused. "Those commitments will not survive what is coming. Nothing this large stays contained indefinitely. The only question is whether we manage the opening or someone else does."

"How does someone end up embedded for a century?" Garner asked.

Renn stood. "The transfer window is narrow. Wright-Patterson security can create a two-hour gap in surveillance coverage. After that, questions get asked. We extract during that window, fly nap-of-the-earth to avoid radar, and deliver directly to the medical facility at Area 51."

Garner was already on his feet, Dale Brown forgotten. "Crew briefing in thirty?"

"Flight deck only. No ground crew. We handle the patient ourselves." She turned toward the door, then paused. "One more thing. He knows he's being extracted. He's lucid, mobile, but weak. Treat him like any other officer being transferred for medical reasons. Professional courtesy, minimal conversation."

After she left, Delaney looked at Garner. "One hundred years. How many wars has he seen? How many friends has he watched die?"

"Most of them," Garner said quietly.

***

Wright-Patterson Air Force Base materialized through the pre-dawn haze as Pandora 2 descended on a heading that kept them away from the main air traffic patterns. Delaney had filed the flight plan as a navigation systems calibration run, routine enough to avoid scrutiny, vague enough to explain any course deviations.

The hangar they were directed to was on the extreme western edge of the facility, separated from the active flight line by a quarter mile of empty tarmac. No other aircraft nearby. No ground personnel visible.

As Garner brought Pandora 2 into a hover and began the vertical descent, Delaney spotted the transport vehicle, a black SUV with government plates, parked beside a service entrance to the hangar. Two figures stood beside it, both in Air Force dress blues.

"Welcoming committee's here," Delaney reported.

The landing was normal. Garner kept the engines at idle while Delaney went through the shutdown checklist for non-essential systems. They wouldn't be there long.

Renn was already moving to the crew door. "I'll handle the transfer protocol. You two prepare the passenger area."

Delaney climbed down first, his boots hitting the oil-stained concrete as two Air Force officers approached. He got his first clear look at them: a colonel and a major, both wearing medical corps insignia. She was a woman with dark hair streaked with gray. Her counterpart was younger, maybe forty, with the careful posture of someone trained not to reveal too much.

"Director Renn," the colonel said. "Colonel Patricia Andrews. This is Major David Kim. We've been coordinating the transfer."

"Appreciated, Colonel. How is he?"

"Stable. Weak, but ambulatory. We've kept him on IV fluids and standard pain management, but ..." She hesitated. "His physical state is responding less effectively than we hoped. Whatever's happening internally, it's beyond our capabilities."

"The medical facility at Groom Lake is prepared," Renn said. "Let's not waste time."

Colonel Andrews gestured toward the SUV. "He's in the vehicle. We thought it best to minimize exposure."

As they approached, the SUV's rear door opened from the inside. A figure emerged, moving slowly.

Delaney gave a slight gasp.

The man appeared to be in his late fifties with distinguished gray hair, a tall frame that carried itself with military bearing despite obvious fatigue. He wore standard Air Force fatigues with colonel's insignia and a name tag that read ERIKSEN.

Colonel Eriksen straightened as he saw Renn. His expression flickered with quiet acknowledgment, as if seeing her confirmed a detail he had known for decades.

"Director," he said, his voice carrying a faint accent that Garner couldn't quite place.

"Colonel Eriksen." Renn's tone was professional but not cold. "We're ready for transport when you are."

"Your service record will reflect medical retirement," Colonel Andrews said quietly. "Full honors, full benefits. The paperwork is already in motion."

Eriksen nodded once. "Appreciated, Patricia. Though I suspect the address on file won't be receiving any correspondence."

"Forwarding arrangements have been made."

As the group moved toward Pandora 2, Delaney found himself walking beside Captain Garner, both maintaining a respectful distance. Garner's expression was neutral, but his eyes tracked Eriksen's movements with the practiced assessment of someone trained to notice details.

The colonel moved with care but without obvious pain. His gait suggested strength held in reserve rather than weakness, like an athlete conserving energy for a longer race. When they reached the ramp, he paused and looked up at the aircraft.

"V-280," he observed. "Impressive machine. Better than the Ospreys I flew."

"You flew V-22s?" Delaney asked before he could stop himself.

Eriksen glanced at him, and for a moment those eyes focused with an intensity that made Delaney feel suddenly transparent.

They climbed aboard. Delaney had configured one of the crew seats with extra cushioning and a reclining mechanism. Eriksen settled into it with visible relief, accepting the safety harness that Garner helped secure.

Colonel Andrews handed Renn a sealed envelope. "His complete medical file. Everything we could document safely. The specialists at Area 51 will need it."

"Understood. Thank you, Colonel."

"Good luck, Director." Andrews stepped back, then turned to Eriksen. "It's been an honor, sir."

"The honor was mine, Patricia. Give my regards to the 445th."

As the officers departed and the ramp was closed, Delaney moved to the cockpit and began the pre-flight sequence. Through the internal camera feed, he could see Renn sitting across from Eriksen, speaking quietly. He couldn't hear the conversation over the engine noise, but something about the way they sat, the similar angle of their heads, the identical set of their shoulders, triggered a thought Delaney immediately pushed away.

"Pre-flight complete," Delaney reported. "Ready for departure."

Garner's hands moved across the controls with practiced precision. "Clear!"

***

The flight profile called for nap-of-the-earth at two hundred feet through rural Ohio, then a gradual climb west of the Mississippi once they were clear of the densely monitored corridor around Wright-Patterson. Garner had the terrain-following engaged and the VEIL Gen 2 active, painting them as a smear of ground clutter on any radar that bothered to look.

He was forty minutes out when the F-16 appeared.

It came in from the north, fast and descending, and made its intention clear on the first pass: a tight bank that put the fighter's nose briefly across Pandora 2's track. A look. Then it came around for a proper intercept position off the port side, close enough that Garner could see the pilot's helmet in the other cockpit.

The radio crackled on the guard frequency. "Unidentified aircraft at low altitude, bearing two-seven-zero, identify yourself."

Garner's cover flight plan was filed for eight thousand feet. Navigation systems calibration. He had no business being at two hundred feet over rural Ohio, and the F-16 pilot knew it.

His options ran out fast. He could climb into the corridor, which would put Pandora 2's silhouette in full daylight profile above the terrain line, visible to anyone below who looked up, and explain nothing about why he had been at two hundred feet to begin with, or he could hold the deck and let the situation develop.

He held.

"Navigation systems calibration, routine," he said into the radio, his voice neutral. "Experiencing intermittent altitude hold failure. Troubleshooting in progress."

A pause on the other end. The F-16 held its position off the port side, pacing him. Garner kept his course and his altitude and his hands loose on the controls.

The fighter pulled ahead and banked. A second pass, this time tighter, low enough that the exhaust heat was visible as a shimmer in the air above the fuselage. The pilot was looking at the aircraft from underneath, logging the silhouette, reading the rotor configuration.

Garner did not vary his heading by a single degree.

In the back, Eriksen would have felt the change in the aircraft's tension, the way the crew went quiet and the radio traffic shifted. If he noticed, he gave no sign. Renn said nothing on the intercom.

The F-16 came back alongside for thirty more seconds, then pulled up and accelerated away to the north.

The radio stayed quiet.

Garner let out a slow breath. Somewhere, a fighter pilot was writing a report about an unidentified low-altitude aircraft with a rotor signature that didn't match anything in his reference cards. That report would go up a chain and hit a desk where someone with the right clearance would file it without comment. The paperwork would exist. The explanation would not.

"Still on profile," Garner said over the intercom, his voice level. "Continuing west."

Delaney's response was two words. "Copy that."

Neither of them mentioned it again.

***

They were an hour west of Ohio when Renn felt a heavy pressure at the edge of her consciousness, a psychic weight that registered in her body before her mind could name it. She had felt ambient telepathic noise before, usually from proximity to Nordic contact. This was different. This was a consciousness flickering, losing its steady signal the way a transmission loses its carrier frequency in bad weather.

It was coming from the cabin behind her.

She turned in her seat. Eriksen's head had dropped forward slightly. The color in his face had changed. An IV line was still in his arm, feeding steadily, but his breathing had shifted to something shallower and less regular than it had been at takeoff.

He was losing ground.

She sat in indecision for a moment. Establishing deliberate contact with a consciousness that was already flickering would cost her. It was not the same as holding a stable connection with a healthy Nordic. A mind in distress did not have clean edges. She would be pushing into something unstable, and whatever she encountered there would not stay neatly contained when she withdrew.

The alternative was to let him manage on his own and watch his readings drop for the next three hours until they reached the medical facility. She did not know how much margin he had. She did not know if he had any.

She unstrapped and moved aft into the cabin.

She sat across from him, close enough to reach him without stretching. He raised his head slowly when he felt her presence. The eyes that met hers were the same pale blue she had seen in photographs her entire life, and in a mirror every morning of hers.

"You don't have to," he said. His accent was more noticeable now, the Norwegian cadences that had softened over a century of American speech pressing back through the fatigue.

"I know," she said.

She placed her hand over his and opened the connection deliberately.

The connection revealed a mind crowded with the weight of a century's worth of memories. A century of accumulated presence does not dim gracefully; it accumulates. The people he had known were still there, organized not by time but by weight, the ones who had mattered most occupying the most space. She saw soldiers whose names she did not know, but whose faces she could see clearly. An officer, young, killed somewhere in Europe in a war that was already history before she was born. A woman who had not been military, whose expression told Renn everything she needed to know and nothing she had the right to ask about.

The loneliness had a particular quality he could feel through the connection: the durable, quiet solitude of a person who had outlived every context that made them who they were, and kept going anyway, because the mission did not end just because everything else did.

Renn steadied the connection and held it, the way you hold a door open against the wind. Nothing was being taken from him; nothing was given. She was simply making the signal stronger, giving his consciousness something stable to organize around while his body worked to stay functional.

After a while, he spoke without opening his eyes.

"Your father described something to me once, after the Kingman crash. An image, clear as a photograph, he said. Of his daughter, though she hadn't been born yet." A pause. "He was certain."

Renn said nothing. She kept the connection steady.

"He told me he'd seen her, how some of us see things that haven't happened yet. He wasn't frightened by it." Eriksen's breathing had evened out. The flickering had settled. "He was glad."

She stayed with him for a long time after that without speaking.

When she finally withdrew the connection, it cost her what she had known it would. She sat back in her seat and pressed her palms flat against her thighs and waited for her own edges to feel solid again.

Eriksen's color had improved. His head was up. He looked at her with those pale eyes and did not say thank you.

"Rest," she said. "We'll be there in two hours."

He closed his eyes.

Renn sat across from him for a few minutes longer, then made her way back to the cockpit. She strapped in and stared at the terrain scrolling below.

Garner glanced over once. He had the pilot's sense of when something significant had happened in the back of his aircraft, even without being able to see it. He did not ask.

Delaney said, after a moment, "You all right?"

"Yes," she said. "Give me a few minutes."

Delaney turned back to his instruments.

After a while, Garner spoke quietly. "You working on anything interesting? That code you were debugging?"

Delaney welcomed the distraction. "Packet sniffer with some pattern recognition. Trying to identify anomalous network traffic that might indicate intrusion attempts."

"Related to the Prometheus operation?"

"More like lessons learned from it. I've been thinking about how they could have tracked us, identified our network signatures. I just want to have the tools to recognize when someone's watching."

Garner made a minor course correction. "Your old Ghost Watch skills are coming in handy."

"Different context, same principles. Find the patterns, identify the threats, stay invisible." Delaney glanced to the rear. "Speaking of staying invisible, a hundred years of rotating identities. The documentation alone must be incredible. Different social security numbers, different birth certificates, different everything."

"Makes you wonder who handles that," Garner said. "There'd have to be people in the system who know how to create the paperwork to maintain the fiction."

"People like whoever calls the shots for Project Mogul," Delaney said quietly.

They flew on in silence for a while.

***

Area 51 appeared on the horizon as the sun climbed toward noon. Delaney adjusted their approach vector, bringing them in from the northwest to avoid the main facility traffic patterns. The Area 51 medical complex sat apart from the central base, connected by underground tunnels but isolated on the surface.

A dedicated landing pad waited, marked only by painted lines on the concrete. A single vehicle sat nearby, a white van with no markings. Two people in civilian clothes stood beside it, waiting.

"The medical staff is expecting us," Renn confirmed through comms. "Direct transfer to the specialized treatment wing."

Garner brought Pandora 2 into a hover, then settled onto the pad with barely a shudder. The moment the skids touched down, Delaney began the shutdown sequence while Garner secured the controls.

In the passenger area, Renn was already helping Eriksen unbuckle. The colonel moved slowly, accepting her assistance without comment. When he stood, he swayed slightly, and Renn steadied him with a hand on his arm.

The gesture was practiced, efficient, but something about it caught Delaney's attention. The way her hand positioned itself on his elbow, the angle of support, the subtle shift of weight. It reminded him of something, though he couldn't say what.

Delaney opened the crew door and deployed the ramp. The two medical personnel approached: a man and a woman, both middle-aged, both moving with the quiet efficiency of people accustomed to handling delicate situations.

"Colonel Eriksen," the woman said. "I'm Dr. Sarah Blake. This is Dr. Michael Voss. We'll be overseeing your treatment."

Eriksen nodded. "Doctors. I appreciate your discretion."

"Our facility specializes in cases that require alternative approaches," Dr. Voss said carefully.

As they helped Eriksen down the ramp, Delaney caught a fragment of conversation.

"Cellular regeneration techniques they've developed," Dr. Blake was saying.

Eriksen stopped walking. For a moment, he just stood there, looking at the desert horizon. Then he turned to look back at Pandora 2, where Renn stood at the top of the ramp.

Their eyes met across the distance. He held her gaze for a moment longer than the situation required, as if confirming something he had been waiting a long time to verify.

In that moment, with the Nevada sun illuminating both faces, Delaney saw what he'd been avoiding seeing all morning: the same luminous eyes that seemed to catch and hold light.

Then Eriksen nodded once and allowed the doctors to guide him toward the van.

Renn remained on the ramp until the van departed, disappearing down a road that led to the entrance. Only then did she turn and climb back into the aircraft.

"Secure all systems," she said quietly. "We're heading back to Mogul."

As Pandora 2 lifted off, Delaney glimpsed the medical facility through the windscreen. Somewhere below, Colonel Eriksen was beginning treatment that could extend his remarkable life.

Another century of watching friends age and die. Another century of rotating through identities, of keeping secrets, of serving a cause that most people didn't know existed.

Delaney thought about the way Eriksen had looked at the landscape on their climb out. The expression of someone saying goodbye to a life, even knowing another waited on the other side.

By the time they landed at S-3, Delaney had added another observation to a growing collection of things he would never voice. Renn secured the cockpit and headed for her office without a word. Captain Garner began the post-flight checklist with his usual methodical precision.

Delaney opened his laptop and stared at the lines of Python code without seeing them. His mind was elsewhere, assembling data points into patterns, as his training had taught him.

Renn's age. Her abilities. The careful way she'd never quite explained her father's background. The resemblance to someone who'd been alive for over two centuries.

The code on his screen blurred. Delaney blinked, saved his work, and closed the laptop.

Some algorithms solved themselves. Others required time, patience, and the wisdom to know when to let the pattern emerge on its own.

He pulled out his tablet and began documenting the flight for the official record: a routine systems test, unremarkable in every way, noteworthy only for its complete lack of noteworthy details.

The perfect mission for Project Mogul.

It was the kind of mission that would remain unacknowledged, its details buried in a file that officially didn't exist.

Chapter Eighteen

Revelation

Captain Garner stood from the table in the Ready Room and said he was heading to the mess kitchen for coffee. He offered to bring some back, but both Delaney and the director shook their heads.

Lieutenant Mark Delaney sat in silence while Director Renn finished her report. She glanced over, picked up on his mood, and asked, "Something on your mind?"

Delaney hesitated. "There are a few things I'm trying to figure out."

"About the last mission?"

"Not exactly. I get why we do what we do, it matters, and I'm glad to be part of it."

"So what's bothering you?"

Delaney let out a breath. "There are things I just don't get. Like that first time, with the crashed saucer. You told us to wait, and then the mother ship showed up. How did you know? Or even more, how did they know?"

She looked at him and asked, "That's what's bugging you?"

"It felt like you could talk to them somehow. But we don't have a radio for that."

Renn leaned forward. She rested her chin on her hand and studied him as if he had finally solved a puzzle.

Delaney continued, "And that Gray alien we rescued somehow knew we were there to help. And there have been other times, too."

She lifted her head. "So how would you explain it?"

Delaney took a moment. "With all due respect, I think there's something you're not telling us. I think you can communicate in your head."

Just then, Captain Garner came back into the room, a fresh coffee in hand. He glanced at the director and looked like he might say something, but then sat down at his desk, sipping coffee as he viewed the conversation.

"So, you think I have special powers, is that it?" Renn asked.

Delaney shook his head. "I'm sorry, I didn't mean to accuse ..."

"It's fine," she said, throwing a quick look at Garner with a smile beginning. "You've had similar questions, haven't you, Captain."

Garner gently set down his coffee mug. "I've had my suspicions. Those headaches before contact. Other things. I just didn't know if I should ask."

Renn allowed a fuller smile. "You're more observant than you let on, Captain." She stood and walked to the window overlooking the hangar bay, her reflection visible in the glass. "But Lieutenant Delaney has asked, and I think he deserves an honest response."

Delaney hadn't expected an answer.

"You're right about the communication," Renn said, still facing the window.

"How?" Delaney asked. His voice was so low that it was nearly lost in the hum of the room.

Director Renn turned to face the pair as she stated, "My mother was human, but my father was not."

Captain Garner cleared his throat. "That explains a lot about how you got this assignment." He picked up his coffee mug and set it down without drinking. "One more question." He looked at her. "Does it change anything about how we run the next mission?"

Renn looked at him for a moment. "No," she said.

"Good," he said.

"In 1953. Kingman, Arizona. The Army was testing an experimental long-range radar. Somehow it brought down a spacecraft. The one survivor of that crash was captured. That was my father." She had both hands flat on the table, the same posture she used when she was walking the team through a mission profile. "He was what is described as a Nordic." She paused. "Not what people picture when they hear 'alien.' Not the eight-foot Tall Whites from the same era's reports. He stood about six feet. If he'd walked past you in a parking lot, you might not have looked twice." She paused. "He was transported to the medical facility at Area 51. My mother was the nurse assigned to his care."

"They allowed ..." Delaney interrupted.

Renn allowed a wry smile. "They recorded everything, of course. The pregnancy, the delivery, the early development. This was Area 51. Nothing went unobserved." She paused. "But my mother was human and the tests read as human. Whatever my father contributed to my biology, it didn't register as anything they recognized. They noted some unusual characteristics in the bloodwork and filed it under anomalous and moved on. A facility running classified programs on alien biology missed what was right in front of them because they were looking for something that looked alien." She paused. "Sadly, my father died when I was very young ... complications from the crash injuries. Human medicine couldn't help."

"How'd they find out about your abilities?" Garner asked.

"One day when I was eight, I visited my mother at work. That was in the nineteen sixties. I told her what the alien patients were feeling. I wasn't even supposed to be in the room. When the facility doctors found out, they decided that was very useful."

Delaney frowned. "So you grew up here."

"Other than a few years in college, I spent almost my whole life inside Area 51. You're right, it's exactly why I have this assignment." She moved back to the table, but remained standing. "When Project Mogul was re-established, they needed someone who could communicate with *the aliens*,"her fingers forming air quotes around the word, "and I was the obvious choice."

"Wait." Delaney paused. "You were eight in the sixties. That's over sixty years ago."

Captain Garner interjected, "From what I have gathered, mostly from science fiction lore, Nordic aliens can sometimes live for hundreds of years. Am I right about that?"

"Close enough, Captain," the director replied, adding with a smile, "That's not a question I answer."

Garner had another question. "The Grays and the Tall Whites communicate differently. I've seen that much. Is it the same channel for you each time?"

Delaney looked up. "That's actually what I want to know too."

"It comes from what I am. The hybrid biology is the mechanism. A fully human mind doesn't have the architecture for it. Neither, apparently, does a fully Nordic one. Whatever the combination produces, that's what makes the connection possible. It's about receiving thoughts, before they become words. Not language, but the intention behind it. With the Nordics it feels almost like conversation. With the Grays it's more like being caught in someone else's dream. Vivid, and not entirely comfortable." She paused. "That's what the headaches are. Some minds push harder than others."

"So now you know," she said. She was still, hands at her sides, watching them.

Nobody spoke for a moment. Garner set his mug down and looked at it. Delaney had stopped pretending to look at anything in particular and was watching Renn directly, the way he watched instrument feeds when he wasn't sure what he was reading but knew it mattered.

Renn held the silence for exactly as long as she chose to. Then she gathered her folder from the table, straightened it against the surface once, and moved toward the door.

"We have work," she said without turning around.

Chapter Nineteen

Disclosure

Mark Delaney woke in his quarters with a warning tight in his gut. Something was off. He trusted it. He checked his phone: 0300 hours. A text from Director Renn, sent four minutes earlier: Ready Room. Now. Flight gear.

He was dressed before he finished reading it.

Garner was already in the corridor, boots on, jacket unzipped. He said nothing. The red-lit hallway said enough.

In the Ready Room, Director Renn was standing at the comms console with her back to the door. The main display showed a global signal map, hundreds of simultaneous transmission anomalies lighting up in overlapping clusters across Europe, the Pacific, and Central Asia.

"Sit down," she said without turning. "Both of you."

They sat.

"Forty minutes ago I received a contact." She turned. Her face was composed in the way it was composed when she had already made a decision and was deciding how much of it to share. "Not through the console. Direct." She touched her temple once, briefly. "They are moving tonight. All of them, coordinated, simultaneous. A response to a launch sequence that is already in progress at three sites. Two land-based, one submarine. The trajectories, if they continue, cross the Pacific."

Delaney felt cold all over. "Are you saying someone actually launched?"

"The sequences are authorized and running. The weapons will not reach their targets." She paused. "They told me that much."

Garner's voice was quiet. "And they're telling us because?"

"Because we are the only human channel they trust to hold the information without acting on it." She looked at him steadily. "We have been ordered to stand down. No intercept, no intervention, no contact with Command until it is over. We watch. We wait. We do not get in the way."

The room was still.

"Captain," Renn said. "I need you in Pandora 2. Engines cold, ready to turn in four minutes. If I change my mind about the stand-down, I need us airborne."

Garner was already on his feet. "Where's the intercept point?"

"There isn't one. That's the order." She held his eyes. "But I want the option."

He nodded once and left.

"Delaney." She moved to the console. "Every government signals network in the Pacific theater is going to start generating noise in the next thirty minutes. I need you to monitor without transmitting. Nothing goes out from this console, nothing gets logged. If Command pings us, you are managing a systems fault. Can you do that?"

"Already on it." He pulled his tablet and began partitioning the outbound channels.

Renn stood at the center of the room and did the thing she had been doing since 0220 hours: she kept the contact open, a thin thread of intention at the edge of her perception, not communication exactly, more the awareness of something very large moving with purpose through the dark.

At 0340, Delaney looked up. "Pacific Command just lost telemetry on the submarine. They're going to DEFCON 2 in the next five minutes. NORAD is already there."

Renn said nothing.

At 0347, every outbound channel on his board flatlined simultaneously. Not a fault. A suppression, clean and total, from outside the system. He stared at it. "Director. I'm not managing the blackout anymore. Something else is."

"I know," she said.

On the main display, the signal anomalies stopped moving and held, fixed points of light spread across three continents, perfectly still.

And then nothing happened.

Delaney reached over and pulled up the news feed on the secondary monitor, volume low. A reporter stood frozen with his hand pressed to his earpiece. Behind him, the lower-third read: GLOBAL MILITARY FORCES ON MAXIMUM READINESS.

"The Pentagon briefing has been delayed again," the reporter said. "Sources describe internal confusion."

Garner's voice came through the intercom from the hangar. "I've got eyes on the field cameras. There are craft on the horizon. Seven, maybe eight. Not moving."

"Hold position," Renn said.

They waited.

At 0412, the signal anomalies on the display began to dissolve, one cluster at a time. The suppression on Delaney's board lifted as quietly as it had arrived. The channels came back clean.

Renn closed her eyes for three seconds. When she opened them she crossed to the intercom. "Captain. Stand down. Secure the aircraft."

A pause. Then: "Copy."

Delaney turned the news feed up. The coverage had broken into chaos, every network running phone footage simultaneously: craft hovering motionless above what were clearly missile installations, their surfaces catching the first grey light of dawn.

Garner came back in from the hangar, his jacket still unzipped. He stood beside Delaney and watched the screen without speaking for a long moment.

"At Malmstrom," he said, quietly, "all ten Minuteman missiles went down right after the UFO report. Engineers swore it was impossible. All the separate systems, all dead at once." He shook his head. "And Vandenberg, '64. The dummy warhead intercepted. Two incidents at Minot. A disc over a Ukrainian site when their controls were hijacked." He looked at the screen. "It was all preparation."

"They've been running the drill for seventy years," Delaney said. "Tonight they ran it for real."

On the monitor, financial alerts scrolled alongside the footage. Crypto collapsing. Nikkei down eighteen percent. European markets suspended.

Renn faced them. "People wanted disclosure. Now they're seeing what comes with it."

"The chain of command," Garner said. "If every government is rewriting the rules tonight, who are we reporting to in the morning?"

Renn said nothing for a moment that lasted longer than any of them counted.

"We wait for orders," she said. "And we adapt."

The alert tone from the comms console cut through the room before she finished the sentence. All three turned. The indicator light steadied. Encrypted priority message, origin: Mogul Command.

Garner glanced at Renn. She crossed the room and pressed her hand to the biometric scanner. The system recognized her. Lines of code moved across the screen. The Ready Room was silent except for the low voice of the news anchor and the hum of the machine.

The message finished decrypting.

Renn read it. She did not move for a moment. Then she stepped back from the console and looked at both of them.

"Our stand-down order is lifted," she said. "Command wants us operational by 0600." She paused. "The containment mission is over. They're giving us something else."

Delaney looked at the screen, where the anchor was saying, with careful steadiness, that the President would address the nation within the hour. "What does that mean? Something else?"

"It means the aliens aren't the problem anymore." Renn picked up her folder from the table and held it up. "We are. They had disabled the weapons. All of them, simultaneously, without hesitation. But the command and control networks were still running. The satellites were still up. The communications infrastructure that had authorized the launch sequence in the first place was completely intact. She did not know yet whether that was an oversight."

She pulled out her phone and typed a single line to Thorne: We need to talk about what they didn't disable. She sent it before she could reconsider.

Behind her, on the monitor, the panel experts were talking over one another. Garner reached over and turned it off.

In the silence, Renn moved toward the door. Garner and Delaney watched her go, and neither of them asked where she was headed, because they both already understood: the old mission was finished, and she was already thinking about the next one.

What Comes Next?

The weapons were disabled. The secret is out.

But the aliens didn't dismantle the launch systems. Director Renn knows why. And somewhere in a newly formed government advisory body, a name from a Site Seven procurement record is already maneuvering for position.

The E-Team's containment mission is finished. What comes next has no protocol, no precedent, and no margin for error.

The aliens aren't the problem. We are.

(To be continued in Book Two)

Please Review!

Thank you for your purchase! Reviews are critically important to authors, helping them reach more readers and improve their work. We'd love to hear your honest feedback. Please take a moment to share your experience by leaving a review where you made the purchase.

If you enjoy this book, I invite you to add it to any relevant Goodreads Listopia lists.

As a fiction reader, you might also like these titles by Tim Trott:

The Psychic Barista: A Collection of Paranormal Cozy Mysteries. This collection is a thrilling mystery anthology that reads like a novel, blending the cozy atmosphere of a small-town coffee shop with supernatural intrigue and dangerous criminal plots. At the heart of the story is Samantha Wilson, a barista at the Brown Bean Coffee Shoppe with a secret psychic gift. She must use her abilities to unravel mysterious plots unfolding in their coastal Georgia town. With its unique blend of paranormal elements, small-town charm, and engaging suspense, it's a must-read.

Short Stories: What If?

Tim Trott's Short Stories brings together suspense, humor, and the unknown, taking readers on a journey across genres and into the unexpected. From mind-reading detective adventures to satirical kingdoms, alien revelations to family secrets, each story brings its own twist. Whether uncovering the hidden truths of human nature or pondering the mysteries of the cosmos, these stories will leave you thinking long after the last page.

Please join the **Advance Readers Committee** at TimTrottWrites.com

About the Author

Tim Trott

Tim Trott is an author, publisher, and creative director based in Central Florida. As the owner of Cyberchute Hosting and Tim Trott Publishing, he develops author-centric platforms and modular workflows that support independent writers in building sustainable careers. His work spans fiction, training materials, and business communication, with a focus on clarity, structure, and reader engagement.

Before turning to fiction full-time, Trott built a national reputation as "The Drone Professor," producing FAA-recognized training resources and publishing several guides for commercial drone operators. His background in broadcasting, instructional design, and digital media informs his approach to storytelling, blending technical precision with character-driven narrative.

Early influences included the Hardy Boys series by Franklin W. Dixon, and the works of Aldous Huxley and Robert Heinlein.

Trott writes across multiple genres, including sci-fi alien thrillers, political suspense, and paranormal mystery. His novels explore the tension between hidden forces and ordinary people pushed into extraordinary circumstances. He also hosts the *@Author to Author* podcast on YouTube, where he interviews writers about craft, process, and the evolving publishing landscape.

Tim Trott invites you to visit his website at TimTrottWrites.com to view the current selection of books.

www.ingramcontent.com/pod-product-compliance
Lightning Source LLC
LaVergne TN
LVHW010703110826
845149LV00014B/3215